D1256379

 This book belongs to

Mrs. Pennington

❖» SALTED «❖
LEMONS

By the same author

Dreams & Drummers
Kelly's Creek
Kick a Stone Home
A Taste of Blackberries
Tough Chauncey
Up and Over

» SALTED «
LEMONS

by Doris Buchanan Smith

Four Winds Press
New York

LIBRARY OF CONGRESS CATALOGING IN PUBLICATION DATA

Smith, Doris Buchanan.
  Salted lemons.

  SUMMARY: Ten-year-old Darby Bannister has
difficulty adjusting to a new environment when
she moves with her family from Washington, D.C.,
to Atlanta in the middle of World War II.
  [1. Moving, Household—Fiction.   2. Prejudices—
Fiction]   I. Title.
PZ7.S64474Sal   [Fic]   80-66250
ISBN 0-590-07666-3

Published by Four Winds Press
A division of Scholastic Magazines, Inc., New York, N.Y.
Copyright © 1980 by Doris Buchanan Smith
All rights reserved
Printed in the United States of America
Library of Congress Catalog Card Number: 80-66250
2   3   4   5   84   83   82   81

For Roy Rogers,
with whom I fell in love
at the Sylvan Theater in 1943

» 1 «

» DARBY BANNISTER looked from her mother to her sister.

"Kyla, will you go to the store and get some bread?" Mother was asking for the second time. Kyla, bent over the desk writing a letter to a friend "back home," did not look up or even acknowledge the question. Darby bit her lip. Kyla was usually the most cooperative one, but she had vowed to move only in body and not in spirit.

"Darby, will you?" Mother asked.

"Sure." Darby had vowed, too, but she was glad to have the chance to escape the muddle of moving in. She took the money from Mother, shook a nickel out of her piggy bank, and skipped out the back door and cater-corner through the narrow woods behind her new house.

"Bread, bread, bread," she chanted, as her feet

shuffled through last year's leaves. Sometimes she got to thinking about things and lost herself in imagination. More than once she'd been sent to the store and forgotten what she'd gone for. So now she chanted to remind herself.

As she crossed the side street, her shoes rasped against the pavement. At the curb she jumped to the sidewalk and landed with both feet. Sidewalks only on one side, she observed, looking back across the street to where there was no sidewalk. On the corner was a sign that read "Atlanta City Limits."

Only two days ago, Thursday, she had lived in Washington, D.C. And now all she had were her memories and two souvenir gifts from her friends there. One was a rabbit's foot, for luck. Dad had joked that it wasn't very lucky for the rabbit. But that didn't keep Darby from loving the soft fur. To her, it would be her own personal very best luck.

The other gift was a large coinlike disk with President Roosevelt for heads and The Little White House for tails. The Little White House, where the president often visited, was at a place in Georgia called Warm Springs. The warm water there was said to be good for his polio-crippled legs.

There was no going back, Darby reasoned.

Daddy had been transferred, so she was stuck in this strange place called Atlanta, Georgia, at least until she was old enough to leave home. That would not be for a long time. Probably, she would like to have new friends in the meantime. Perhaps she'd meet her first new friend at the store.

Jingling the money in her pocket, she stopped to read the black lettering on the glass storefront. "Kaigler's Grocery." A metal bar across the door advertised Colonial Bread. Darby pushed against it to enter the dim and unfamiliar store.

"Colonel Bread," she said, misreading the sign. "That's the kind I'll get." *Colonel* was one of those strange words that didn't sound like they were spelled. Once she had looked up the word *colonel* and found that it originally meant "leader of a column," but she had never found out why it was pronounced "kernel."

Inside the store her eyes searched out the candy case and she crossed the worn plank floor to it. Behind the glass was a mind-boggling array of penny candy. There were Mary Janes, Tootsie Rolls, silver bells, peppermint sticks, jaw breakers, and long, twisted ropes of licorice, all for a penny each. Even better were the gum drops, jelly beans, and licorice stars, which were five for a penny. The display of candy was almost identical to that in the neighborhood store in Washington, D.C.

"Eh, *Blümchen?* Make up your mind," a gravelly voice said. Startled, Darby looked up into a face rumpled enough to match the voice.

"Uh . . . uh . . ." she said, hesitating a minute, flustered, unable to choose. "Uh, five peppermint sticks," she said, naming her standby, "and, uh, a loaf of Colonel Bread."

"Colonel Bread, eh?" the man said, as he stuffed five peppermint sticks into a small bag. His graying hair was as wild and unruly as his eyebrows, and he spoke with some kind of foreign accent. "One loaf of Colonel Bread," he said, plucking it from a shelf and setting it on the counter along with the sack of peppermints. He held out his thick hand for the money, but Darby, not daring to touch him, plunked the money on the counter.

"What's your name?" she asked, looking straight at his face to prove she wasn't afraid of him.

"Kaigler," he said. "What's yours, *Blümchen?*"

"Darby," she said, picking up her candy and the bread. With her chin held high she turned her back on him, knowing that as soon as she emerged from his dusky store she would feel like Queen of the World.

Several laughing children came through the door together. Holding her precious goods close for security, Darby looked right at them, half smiling and ready to speak. They would be her first friends. They, however, saw only the candy case and didn't even notice her. She tried not to mind. Just any old body couldn't speak to the Queen of the World, anyway.

One of the smaller children pointed to the colors on the door bar. "That's yellow and that's red and that's blue," she said. "What does it say?"

"It says, 'Colonial is good bread,' " an older boy said.

"It says, 'Colonel is good bread,' " Darby said, before she could stop herself.

"What?" the boy asked. "What does it say?"

"Colonel," she said, feeling just like a teacher, which is what she thought she would be when she grew up. "Even though it says c-o-l-o-n-e-l, it is pronounced like kernel."

"There's no r," the boy said. "And what about that i there? That i-a-l?"

Darby hadn't noticed that, the i-a-l. "Oh," she said. "Then it's kernial."

All at once things exploded. The storekeeper barked for them to shut the door, because they were letting in flies, and the boy hollered and held his stomach, saying, "Hey, y'all. Did you hear what she said? Kernial!"

"It is kernial. Kernial Bread," Darby said, touching the loaf under her arm. "I have some right here so I ought to know." Hadn't Mr. Kaigler said "kernial," too?

"Kernial! Ha, ha!" All the children were laughing now, even the little one whom she'd tried to help so she wouldn't learn the word wrong.

"And did you hear her accent? She's a Yankee. Yankees sure must be dumb."

"A freckle-faced Yankee!"

By that time they had exchanged places through the doorway, and she was on the hot September sidewalk and they were inside, still laughing. They let the door swing closed with a bang.

Yankee? Dumb? What sort of horrible place was this Atlanta, Georgia? She glanced into the glass storefront to see her reflection. She looked the same as always, short blonde hair, blue eyes. She had not turned into a wart-faced monster. The word *Yankee* was not printed across her forehead.

The heat rose from the sidewalk and set her face on fire. Extending her lower lip, she blew upward to cool her face, as she looked about her. A boy came running down the street. Without stopping, he threw something at the store window and shouted, "Old man Kaigler is a spy!"

Darby spun her head to look at the store window. What had hit with a splat was a raw egg. The yellow yolk was oozing down the window. The sight of it made her sick.

Darby didn't want to go home with her face full

of embarrassment, and she couldn't keep standing in front of the store. Those horrid children would be coming out in a minute. Horrid children. Strange, thick-tongued storekeepers. Spies. What kind of a place was this? Half a block up and across the street she saw the school. Instead of heading home, she walked in the opposite direction, toward the school, licking the end of a peppermint stick.

The school was a two-story building, tall and square and forbidding, towering over the street right at the edge of the sidewalk. Her old school had been low and long and back from the road, nestled in a grove of trees. As her face cooled, she stood staring at the building, willing it to look comfortable and inviting.

On Monday I'll be there, she thought, wondering which were the windows of the fifth-grade classrooms. Would any of those store children be in her class? She hoped not. When she walked back past the store, Mr. Kaigler was out front washing the window.

"There are all kinds of people in the world, *Blümchen*," he said. But he seemed to be talking more to himself than to her, so she hurried past. By the time she got home, a half block the other way from the store, her peppermint was licked to a fine point.

"What took you so long?" Mother asked, as

Darby put the bread on the kitchen table. Darby shared peppermints with Kyla and Blair, her older and younger sisters, and with Mom and Dad. She wished she had another for herself. She sucked air into her mouth so the coolness would linger.

"I went down to look at the school," she said, keeping her hand on the loaf of bread to remind herself to ask the question. Besides trying to make the school feel warm and familiar, she had sort of hoped someone would notice her, maybe, and come up and say, "I go to that school. Are you new here?"

"What school?" Mother asked, as she popped the end of the peppermint stick in her mouth. Dad crunched his and it was gone in a minute.

"What school?" Darby said, frowning. "What school do you think? The one down from the store. My school. Our school," she said, including Kyla, who would be in sixth grade.

"That's not our school, dumbo," Kyla said.

"What do you mean, not our school?" Her eyes spit fire at Miss Know-it-all Kyla.

"She's right, Darby," Mom said. "That's not where you and Kyla are going to school."

Darby grimaced. Of course she's right. Wasn't Miss Kyla Marie Bannister always right?

"The school down from the store is the city school," Dad said. "Deckner Avenue, the street between here and the store, is the boundary of the city limits. We're a half block into the county. You and Kyla will be going to Perkerson School, about a mile the other way." Dad pointed out across the screened porch to indicate the direction.

"What?" Darby said. "I thought we lived in Atlanta. I even saw the sign." She felt betrayed.

"We live a half block on the wrong side of the sign," Dad said, laughing as though it were a huge joke.

"Going to a school a mile away when there is one right out the back door doesn't make a bit of sense," she protested. "What kind of stupid place is this, anyway?" Why had they told her they were moving to Atlanta if they were going to live out of Atlanta? She'd told all her friends she was moving to Atlanta.

The whole situation was growing more complicated every minute. Darby was finding it hard not to behave like three-year-old Blair, who wailed every night to "go home." Home was Washington, where their house was two stories instead of one, and the school was one story instead of two, and there were friends and cousins and familiar streets. Oh, there were so many reasons they should have stayed in Washington.

A couple of years ago Dad had taught her a way of making decisions. "List the reasons for making the decision on the left-hand side of the paper and the reasons against on the right-hand side," he had said. "Usually, you should choose the side with the longest list."

When she'd wanted a dog, Darby had naturally come up with more reasons for getting one than for not getting one. And even though he didn't want her to have a dog, Dad had not questioned her decision. That was when she got Blackie Dog.

Blackie Dog had disappeared a few weeks before they moved. It was as though he knew they were going to move and didn't want to go. She hadn't wanted to go, either, but she didn't know how to disappear, and Dad had not accepted her list against moving.

With her hand still on the loaf of bread, she asked, "Do you see what kind of bread this is?"

Turning from the counter where she was wiping dishes and putting them in the cabinet, Mother said, "Hmmm. Colonial. Colonial Bread."

Colonial, like colonist, Darby thought. Like colonial times, Jamestown and Plymouth Rock and coming over on the Mayflower. She knew *colonial.* How had she made such a mistake? The heat rose in her face again at the thought of herself saying "kernial" to that bunch of rude, laughing children.

"See?" Blair said. "I'm being a careful helper." Blair was unwrapping things and setting them on the table. Kyla and Dad had gone to set up beds, so they wouldn't have to sleep again on mattresses on the floor.

Darby reached into a barrel and unwrapped a glass swan. "Mmm," she said to Blair, to cover her renewed embarrassment. "You're being a big helper." She was no swan, she thought, as she set the ornament down on the table. She was more like an ugly duckling.

❖❯ 2 ❮❖

❖❯ AFTER DINNER, Daddy took them for a walk to see their school. Darby insisted she didn't want to see the dumb old school, but she was glad for a chance to get out. Kyla, who was interested neither in the school nor a walk, had to be coaxed, but Dad was a strong persuader. They followed him through the thin woods behind the house and turned their backs on the other school, the store, and the City Limits sign. Because of the war gas was rationed, and cars were used only for important things.

"When cars are coming, you get out of the road and over at least four feet," Dad said, moving over into the brush to show them the distance he meant. "And you do it whether anyone else does or not," he said. "You never know when a driver is going to be careless." There were sidewalks in the city, Darby noted, but nothing but curbs and scrubby woods along here. The long black road rose steeply ahead.

"How much farther?" Darby asked, as they pushed up the hill.

"Oh, not much," Dad said, striding along at his own pace and leaving it up to them to keep up. If she were still little, like Blair, he would scoop her up and lift her to his shoulder, carrying her along as if she weighed nothing at all. But being ten meant weighing a lot more than Blair, and though he was tall and immensely strong, Dad never carried her on his shoulders anymore except at the pool. There, she would climb to his shoulders as he crouched in the water, and when he rose, she would dive.

"Daddy, am I a Yankee?" she asked, as they tramped onward.

"Well, yes and no, depending on how you mean it," he said. "Our soldiers overseas are called Yanks, for Yankees, because they are Americans. So, in that sense, all Americans are Yankees. Then again, there is an imaginary line between Maryland and Pennsylvania called the Mason and Dixon line. This line divides the north from the south. Northerners, people who live above the line, are often referred to as Yankees. In this sense, being from Washington, D.C., you are not a Yankee."

"What's wrong with being a Yankee?" she asked,

looking up the hill, relieved to see they were nearing the top.

"Oh, what makes you think there is anything wrong with being a Yankee?"

"Well," she said quietly, not liking to think of how hateful they had sounded when they said it, "they called me one."

"They?"

"Some kids at the store."

"Well, don't you mind. You know about sticks and stones, don't you? Your voice sounds a little strange to them, just as theirs probably does to you."

Mr. Kaigler had the strangest voice of all, she thought.

"An accent doesn't have a thing to do with what kind of person someone is," Dad continued. "And as for being a Yankee, one part of the country is just as good as another."

"And they say the man at the store is a spy," she said, stretching the truth. "They" hadn't said it; the boy running was the only one who had said it.

"They who, lamb?"

"The kids. A boy threw an egg at the store window."

"That was an awful thing to do," he said. "I wouldn't pay any attention to what people like that say if I were you." His assurance was comforting.

Finally the whole hill was under them, and Dad pointed to a traffic light ahead, where they would turn right toward the school. After turning, they saw more woods on their right, tall, thick, green woods that reminded Darby of Rock Creek Park in Washington. And when she saw the school, she thought it was worth every step of the walk. It was one story, low and long and nestled back in the trees. She had no trouble at all making this school look warm and welcoming.

⋄» 3 «⋄

» ON SUNDAY MORNING, Darby, Mother, Blair, and Kyla all dressed and marched into the September sunshine to Sunday school. Darby wanted to stay home with Dad, who spent his Sunday mornings with the newspaper. After her experience at the store yesterday, she was no longer anxious to meet these Georgia people.

They walked out of the county, where there were no sidewalks, and onto the city sidewalks. Did the city people feel special, having sidewalks? Darby wondered. Two blocks up, their street ended at an intersection with another, and straight across was the Methodist church with a tall steeple.

The girls followed Mother down narrow side stairs and into a basement room with brown and black checkerboard tile on the floor. Mother introduced Darby and Kyla to the superintendent of the department. Then, taking Blair by the hand, she left them. Darby felt more alone in this room full of strangers than she would have felt standing outside by herself.

"We're glad to welcome two visitors today," the superintendent said when everyone had sat down. "Kyla and Darby Bannister, who live down on Athens Avenue. Kyla and Darby, will you stand?" The woman raised her arm as though to lift them magnetically from their chairs. Kyla wouldn't stand, and Darby wouldn't stand without Kyla. They poked at each other until finally, together, they stood.

"Do you live on old Athens or new Athens?" the woman asked. Darby and Kyla looked at each other and shrugged. "What's the house number?" she asked. Darby gave it, and the woman nodded. "Yes, that's new Athens." The wrong side of the City Limits sign, Darby thought.

"Now," said the superintendent, "in preparation for our contest, which will begin next week, we'll divide into teams." One of the teachers went up and down the rows, counting to four repeatedly. Then he designated places for the group of each number to stand. Darby, who was a two, followed Kyla.

"You're not a three," Kyla said, pushing Darby toward the two line. Darby joined the twos reluctantly. In this whole room of moving people, Kyla was the only person she knew.

"Are you a Yankee?" a boy on her team asked. The question surprised her because she hadn't even said a word. Was he one of the tormenters of yesterday?

"No," she said. "I'm not a Yankee. I'm from Washington, D.C."

"She's a Yankee," someone else said.

Shaking her head, she explained about the imaginary line.

"Imaginary line?" another said. "Yeah, sure, imaginary. You imagined it right up there in your dumb Yankee head!"

The groups were breaking up to go into separate classrooms. Darby looked around for Kyla, but Kyla had disappeared. Totally abandoned, she thought to go home. But she wasn't sure she could find her way when she felt like this. How had these imaginary lines—Mason-Dixon, city-county—suddenly invaded her life? How awful it was to be a stranger.

A teacher stood in a doorway, beckoning to Darby. Not knowing what else to do, she went.

The strange faces in the classroom blurred together, so Darby concentrated on the objects in the room instead. The walls were pale yellow, and there were white curtains on the window. The white chairs had yellow covers over the backs, like shawls.

"Now, don't forget about the contest," the teacher said when the lesson was over. Contest? Darby had already forgotten about the contest, and she hadn't listened to the lesson.

During the afternoon, Darby remembered a little bit about the contest. Points were to be given for certain things, like learning the books of the Bible, memorizing verses, and reading chapters.

"Six months? Did they say six months?" she asked Kyla.

"Six months what?" Kyla said impatiently, looking up from a book.

"The Sunday school contest."

"Yes, six months," Kyla said, returning to her reading.

Darby loved contests, and she was a whiz at reading and memorizing. She would get a lot of points for her team, and they would all like her. With Bible and pencil and tablet in hand, she crawled onto the top bunk and lay on her stomach. I wonder if I can read the whole Bible in six months, she thought.

Using one of Dad's organizing methods, she began to figure. If you had a book you wanted to read in a certain number of days, Dad said you should divide the number of pages by the number of days, and you would know how many pages to read each day. She counted the books in the index of the Bible. There were thirty-nine books in the Old Testament and twenty-seven in the New. If she read a book a day, she could read it all in sixty-six days and maybe do it again before the six months were up.

All afternoon she read, changing positions from time to time for comfort. She read through the creation and Adam and Eve and Noah and Joseph, and she still hadn't finished Genesis. Flipping through the thin pages, she discovered with horror that Genesis had fifty chapters. She collapsed with a huge sigh.

For fresh air and diversion, she took her Bible out to the narrow woods behind the house. Finding just the right tree, she sat down with her back comfortably against it, facing away from the house. She resumed reading. Occasionally a car wooshed along Stewart Avenue and she looked up. She was trying to learn the difference in cars, but the only one she really knew was the round-backed Ford, like Daddy's.

Across the way a door slammed, and Darby looked up again. A girl about her age was on the porch of the house across Stewart. Darby had noticed the house because it had a basket swing hanging on the porch. As she watched, the girl walked through the front yard to the curb. Was she coming to play in the woods?

Yesterday Darby had been anxious for a friend, but today she was busy. She decided to pretend she was invisible. As the girl crossed the street and walked straight toward her, Darby clutched her arms around her shins and stared at her feet. In a moment the girl's feet came into her line of vision.

"Hey, I'm Yoko Sasaki," the girl said. "I live over there." Darby didn't look up, but she knew the girl was pointing to the white house with the basket swing. "Do you want a lemon?" This time Darby looked up to see what the girl had meant. She had meant, "Do you want a lemon?"

"They're good," the girl said. In one hand she had two halves of a lemon. She had a salt shaker in the other hand. After shaking salt over one half, she put it to her mouth and sank her teeth in without even making a face.

"Isn't it sour?" Darby asked, wondering what kind of name Yoko was, what kind of girl she was. Her skin was the color of taffy and her short bobbed hair was the shiniest black, blue-black like coal. Was she Chinese? Filipino?

"Mmmm. Good and delicious sour," Yoko said. She salted the second half and handed it to Darby. "Here. Try it."

The lemon was sliced lengthwise, which made it

look as though it had only two sections, instead of the many sections that showed up when Mother cut a lemon. When Darby sank her teeth into it, the juice ran onto her tongue and sour sparks shot through her head and out through her ears. "Mmmm," she said, wrinkling her face. "Good. More salt." She held out the lemon to Yoko, and Yoko added salt.

"I heard the kids talking mean to you yesterday," Yoko said, sitting down beside Darby. Darby shrugged.

"You did? Where are you from?" They were both outsiders. That was why Yoko was being friendly.

"I'm from here," Yoko said. "I was born right here and have lived my whole life in that house." Yoko sounded defiant.

Darby tried not to stare. The black hair was blacker than any other black hair she had ever seen. Her own hair was cut in the same type of bob and Darby hated it, but Yoko's hair looked just right. "Aren't you Chinese, or something?" Darby asked.

"I'm a rebel," Yoko said.

"What's a rebel?" Darby asked.

"A rebel is a southerner," Yoko explained. "Someone from the southern states."

"Then I must be a rebel, too," Darby said.

"You don't sound like one. Where did you move from?"

"I moved from a city but not from a state," Darby said, using Dad's old riddle.

"Oh, from another country?" Yoko asked with excitement.

"No. I already told you I was a rebel," Darby said, and she explained about the imaginary line between Maryland and Pennsylvania. "I'm from Washington, D.C."

"Did you hate to move? I'd hate to move. I can't imagine living anyplace else."

Darby nodded. It was hard for her to look at Yoko's foreign face and think that she was born right here.

"I had this dog named Blackie Dog who got lost just a few weeks before we moved," Darby said. What would it be like to have never moved, she wondered. She had moved twice before, but just in Washington. She'd never had to come such a long distance away from the place she considered home. "We looked for him everywhere but couldn't find him, and I could hardly bear to leave without him." She had a lot more against moving than leaving Blackie Dog, but it was easier to talk about him than some of the other things, such as leaving her friends and her grandmother and the very ground that was so familiar. Even as they were driving away, she'd looked out the back window for miles, expecting to see Blackie Dog come running along behind.

"I have a dog named Muffin," Yoko said. "He looks just like a mop, all short and furry. His tail fluffs up so that you can hardly tell which end of him is which." They both laughed. Darby scraped her teeth against the rind of the lemon. "I know I'd hate it if anything happened to Muffin. I'd hate it even worse than moving, and you had to have both."

"Yeah," Darby said. Yoko was a person who understood.

"Maybe you can get another dog."

"No. I doubt it," Darby said. "Dad hates dogs." Saying it out loud made her realize how much he loved her. Even though he didn't like dogs, he'd let her have Blackie Dog. And when Blackie Dog got lost, he had walked with her for miles, up and down streets, calling and looking and asking. Then Dad had taken her in the car, gas rationing and all, to search some more.

"What kind of shoes are those?" Darby asked, looking at the tan, woven shoes that Yoko wore without socks. The shoes reminded Darby of the basket swing.

"They're huaraches," Yoko said. "They're from Mexico, and they're the most comfortable shoes

I've ever had. Like them?" Yoko held out one foot for more detailed inspection.

"Oh, yes," Darby said, in awe of a girl who wore shoes without socks. Mother didn't allow her to go without socks. Huaraches! And from Mexico! How exotic.

"Are you from Mexico?" Darby asked, not really thinking Yoko was from Mexico. Mexicans were more Indian looking, Darby thought, though her experience with Mexicans and Orientals was limited to geography books.

"No, I told you. I'm from here. I'm a Georgian."

Darby puzzled over the word, as she continued gazing at the shoes. They had a nifty little pull tab at the heel. She already had her shoes for this year, but maybe next spring she could have some huaraches. Her hair would be grown out, too. Wouldn't she be the Queen of the World for sure with long hair on her head and huaraches on her feet?

"What's a Georgian?" Darby asked.

"Someone from Georgia," Yoko said, and Darby felt like a dumbo again. Kyla was right. For all her good grades in school, she was a dumbo.

Later, Darby told Mother about Yoko, about having a friend from the neighborhood and a friend to walk to school with.

"I'm so glad you have a friend," Mother said,

hugging her. "But I don't think she will be going to school with you."

Darby looked at her mother, perplexed. "Where else would she go? She lives in the county."

"Ah . . . um . . . sweetheart, I'm afraid she lives in the city." Mother reached out to hug Darby again, but Darby jerked away.

"Her house is right behind ours," Darby said, stomping her foot and pointing through the window, through the narrow woods and across Stewart Avenue to the white house with the reddish brown shutters.

Mother shook her head sadly. "The city limits come down Deckner, across Stewart, and go south to just past Yoko's house."

"Just because they have a sidewalk doesn't mean it's city." All this city-county business was getting to be too much.

"In this case, darling, I'm afraid it does."

Darby pressed her lips together and narrowed her eyes. She was beginning to hate sidewalks. "I don't believe you," she said to her mother. "You just don't want me to have any friends."

"You can still be friends, Darby," Mother said. "You just won't go to the same school. And please don't talk to me in that tone of voice."

"How can we be friends if she's with those people who call me Yankee and if we don't go to the same school? We won't be able to walk together, and we won't hardly ever see each other." She ran from the room, hurtled herself onto the top bunk, and sobbed until the bed bounced and she smelled the salt from her tears and her breath was coming in see-saw gasps.

» 4 «

» MOTHER WAS RIGHT about Yoko. As they
waited in front of Kaigler's store for the bus
that would take them to Perkerson school, Yoko
passed by on the other side of the street, going
one block to her school. Yoko waved and Darby
waved. Blair waved, too.

"It doesn't make sense," Darby said, watching
Yoko disappear into the tall brick schoolhouse.
She thought she would like to kick down that City
Limits sign.

A boy with a round face limped up to the bus
stop from behind them. Darby looked at him with
interest, wondering if he lived near her. He returned the look of interest and she half expected
him to say, "Are you the new girl?" But he said
nothing.

When the bus came, Darby took Blair's hand

28

and boosted her up the steep steps. Blair was the reason they were riding the bus instead of walking. Mother didn't have anyone to baby-sit yet. The boy, who sat on the front seat behind the driver, was probably riding because he'd hurt his leg, Darby guessed.

They journeyed up the child-filled walkway to register for school. To their surprise, they learned that Perkerson School had never heard of Kyla and Darby Bannister.

"But I had their records sent ahead," Mother said. From the school office, Mother called long distance to Washington.

"Tell them to say hello to Joyce, Bernie, Mary, and Joel," Darby said, pulling on Mother's sleeve. Mother motioned for her to hush.

"They say the records were mailed a week before we even left," Mother said.

"We could wait a few days to see if they come," the principal said.

"I don't like for them to miss that much school," Mother said.

"Well, if you bring them back at three o'clock, we can give them entrance tests."

"Entrance tests?" Darby asked when they left the school.

"Yes, so they'll know what grade to place you in."

"But we know what grade to go in."

"Yeah, dumbo, but they can't just take our word for it," Kyla said. "You could walk in and say sixth grade, and I could say eighth."

"It's okay for you to be smart about it," Darby said. She didn't miss the fact that Kyla, in her example, had put Darby one grade ahead and put herself two grades ahead. Easy enough for her, who glided over schoolwork like skates on ice, but Darby had to work to do well. And now she wouldn't even be able to study, because she had no idea what the questions would be.

Just before three o'clock that afternoon, they waited again for the bus on the city corner in front of Kaigler's store. But now there was no Yoko to give a friendly wave. Darby hated it when they got off the bus and walked against the tide of children leaving school.

"I'll wind up back in fourth grade, I know I will," she complained, as they approached the school.

"Oh, quit worrying," Kyla said. "You'll do fine."

"Sure you will," Mother said. "You're every bit as smart as Kyla." Kyla was smart all right, but the words didn't reassure Darby. She made good grades, and they said she was smart, but she felt like a clunkhead. Colonel Clunkhead, she thought grimly.

From the principal's office, Kyla was sent down

the hall with a sixth-grade teacher and Darby with a fifth-grade teacher. Darby followed the teacher into an empty classroom.

"I'm Miss Hardy, and I'll be your teacher," Miss Hardy said, as she handed Darby some papers and a sharp pencil. Miss Hardy was taking a lot for granted, Darby thought, wishing she were in a crowded place and not alone in this empty room with her barren brain. It's my own private test, she thought, trying to think of herself as Queen of the World, who couldn't take tests in crowded places with the peons.

"Don't be worried," Miss Hardy said. "It's just some fourth-grade work in language and geography and arithmetic. Let me know when you're finished, and I'll give you some spelling."

Darby bent over the papers, sure that she would be struck with sudden blindness. "I'm so very sorry," she would have to say to Miss Hardy, "but something is wrong with my eyes." She would be noble and brave and they would all huddle around and be sorry for her. How sad for the Queen of the World to go blind. And so young, too.

"Underline the pronouns in the following sentences," the first direction said.

"Oh, pronouns," Darby thought. "That's easy enough." The next set of sentences were for subject and predicate, also easy. The arithmetic was harder. When she saw fractions she nearly gulped her tonsils.

The geography was pretty easy, too, though she was humiliated at the sight of the word *colonial.* There were questions about the colonies and she had to list all thirteen. There were six colonies below Pennsylvania, which meant seven colonies were Yankee colonies. Maybe she would ask Miss Hardy about the Mason and Dixon line.

When she was finished, Miss Hardy took her papers. Then she opened a spelling book. She read the words to Darby, who wrote each one on her paper.

Spelling was one of Darby's best subjects, and she zipped through the list until she came to the last word. *Radio.* R-a-d-i-o went through her head immediately, but before she wrote it, she decided it was *rodeo* that ended with *i-o. Radio* ends with an *e-o,* she thought. As many times as she'd read the radio listing schedule in the paper, she still couldn't be sure. Was it *i-o* or *e-o?* Miss Hardy was waiting.

"*I-o* or *e-o,*" she said aloud. "One goes with *radio,* and one goes with *rodeo,* but I can't re-member which."

"Take your time," Miss Hardy said. "Which one do you think?"

Dad said that with spelling, your first impression is usually right. But now Darby couldn't remember which had been her first impression. The image of a cowboy bucking up and down on a bronco came to mind, and with it came the certainty that *rodeo* was spelled *r-o-d-i-o.*

"*E-o,*" she said. "*Radio, r-a-d-e-o, radio.* That's how we were taught to spell. Say the word, then spell it, then say it again. Is that the way you do it here?" Committed, she wrote *r-a-d-e-o* on her paper.

"Exactly, Darby," Miss Hardy said, taking the spelling paper and looking at it. "Except that you didn't spell *radio* exactly."

"I didn't?" Her eyes flew wide with embarrassed surprise.

"That's the only one you missed, though, so you did just fine. If you want, you may look around the room while I check over your other papers."

Darby nodded and stood up. Dumbo. Kyla would be sure to say it when she found out. Darby strolled around the room, not really seeing anything, until a large construction-paper map on the bulletin board caught her attention. Each state was cut out separately and pinned to the bulletin board. Oh, yeah, she thought, feeling a little at home. The fifth grade always studies states and capitals. Probably Miss Hardy took the map off the bulletin board, scrambled it up, and had them put it together again. She smiled. She and Kyla played the game of states all the time. She already knew

most of the states and capitals. At the window, she
saw Mom out back, swinging Blair. She knocked
on the window and motioned for them to come.

"Well, miss, you are a bright young lady," Miss
Hardy said. "You missed only *radio.*"

"I know," Darby said. "You told me."

"I mean out of everything. Out of your whole
test, you missed only *radio.*"

"Really?" Darby said, so quietly that the sound
almost didn't come out.

"I'll go tell the principal," Miss Hardy said.
"You'll be in my fifth-grade class, and I will be
delighted to have you."

Shortly, Mother came down the hall with Kyla
and Blair. Joy rose in her, but Darby held it down
because it wasn't proper to boast. To keep from
shouting, she kept her lips pressed between her
teeth.

As Mother went into the principal's office,
Darby took Blair by the hand and walked down
the hall. It was all she could do to keep from
hugging herself. How much better to have someone else say nice things about you than to have to
say them yourself.

"We'll wait out front," Darby said. But nosy Kyla
stayed right there. Well, Kyla would find out who
wasn't a dumbo. At the front stairs, Darby lifted
Blair and held her in a straddle on the railing, letting her slide down.

"Did you ever see a Bannister slide down a bannister?" she asked, laughing, as she carried Blair to the top of the stairs so she could slide again.

"And did you ever see butter fly? Or a board walk?"

Mother and Kyla came through the doorway, the principal following and waving good-bye.

"Did you ever see a chimney sweep?" Darby said happily to Kyla and Mother. Giddiness was overcoming her.

Halfway down the walkway, she glanced back at the school building to see if they were out of hearing distance. It wasn't bragging to talk about good things to your own family, Mother and Dad both said.

"Did she tell you?" she asked. "Did she tell you?" Blair had run ahead and was standing by the three steps down to the sidewalk, where there was another short railing.

"Do me, do me," she said. "Slide me. Bannister on the bannister."

"Oh, my darling, yes, certainly. I'm so proud of you!" Mother pulled her close in a quick hug.

Lifting Blair, Darby slid her down the bannister, then straddled it herself for the short ride. Short as it was, however, the ride was long enough to draw Darby's joy bubble to the surface.

"How did you do, Kyla? I'll bet you made a hundred. I'll bet you nearly made their eyes pop out!"

Arms out, Darby twirled as she talked. "I'll bet they've never had anyone make a hundred on an entrance test before, and I almost made a hundred. We'll be Queens of the World!"

"Will you please shut up!" Kyla said abruptly.

Darby shut her mouth as though it had a spring on it. She looked at Blair, running ahead and happily reciting nursery rhymes, one after the other. Kyla stopped walking and let Darby and Mother go ahead. Slowly it burrowed into Darby's head that Kyla had not added the usual "dumbo" to her remark. So that was it. She had done better than Kyla on the tests, and Kyla couldn't stand it. Kyla must have missed two questions.

"Oh, I get it," Darby said to Mother, taking long steps to match her mother's and imagining her feet in huaraches. "For once I did better than Kyla at something, and she can't stand it. Boy, am I going to have fun with this." She flounced around and took a step toward Kyla, who was plodding, long faced, and scuffing her shoes on the dirt path. A sudden pain in her shoulder stopped her short.

"Whaaa?" she cried out. Mother had a mule-bite grip on her shoulder.

"You'll do nothing of the kind," Mother said.

"How come?" Darby said, glancing back at Kyla. "I was just going to call her dumbo. She calls me dumbo all the time."

"Sweetheart, I am very proud of you, but Kyla didn't do well on the test, and she's upset about it. You can understand that, can't you? Blair, come back, now." Blair was far ahead and approaching the intersection.

"So? Just because she didn't make a hundred or something. What did she make? Eighty-eight?"

"Let's just not talk about it, okay?" Mother said, putting her arm around Darby's waist.

Blair started back toward them, singing, "There was a man in our town, and he was wondrous wise."

"Golly, you act like she failed or something," Darby said. "I don't care what you say, I'm going to call her dumbo." Turning quickly, she cupped her hands around her mouth and shouted, "Kyla is a dumbo."

"Darby, stop." Mother jerked Darby's arm. "Leave her alone. She's miserable enough without your rubbing it in. She *did* fail."

"She what?" Darby said, though the words were clear and clanging in her ear.

"She didn't pass her tests," Mother said quietly, glancing back to be sure Kyla didn't hear. "She's going to have to go into fifth grade instead of sixth."

Darby's mouth fell open, and pain rushed through her.

"I'll get Blair," she said suddenly, and she ran

ahead, scooped up the baby, and twirled her around, increasing the distance between them and Mother, them and Kyla. Kyla would be in fifth grade with her?

"There was a man in our town, and he was wondrous wise," Blair sang. "He jumped into a bramble bush and scratched out both his eyes."

Poor Kyla. She must feel as if her own eyes had been scratched out. How could she bear it? The "man of our town" jumped back into the bramble bush and scratched his eyes in again. But how could Kyla ever get her eyes back? How awful to be older and smarter than your sister, and wind up failing and being put in the same grade with her.

Darby glanced back and saw Kyla still trudging along. To Darby, it was the bravest sight she'd ever seen.

∴» 5 «∴

»∴ AT HOME, Kyla closed herself inside their
room, and Darby retreated to the front steps.
Like Kyla, she needed to be alone. But Kyla had
claimed the bedroom and Blair was playing on the
screened porch. And if she went to the woods to
sit, Yoko might see her and come over. On the
front steps she was absolutely alone, because nothing was moving, up or down the street.

Sometimes Darby played a game with herself.
She pretended to be another person and tried to
imagine what the person thought and felt. She was
trying to be Kyla now, and there was a black, bot-
tomless hole inside herself. She just couldn't sum-
mon up an image for what Kyla must be feeling.

Darby had already imagined herself as Blair and
knew how it was to be three years old and not understand about moving, and to be crying to go

39

home. Home. Home was where Blair had a high upstairs window next to her bed, and a grandmother called Mimmie to hold her in her lap, rocking her and reading her stories, and to wash her all soapy in the bathtub and rub her back until she fell asleep. Home was where Blair could sit on the landing of the staircase and play, pretending it was her own special small house. But Darby could not imagine enough to be Kyla.

From around the corner, a boy and girl came walking. The boy was the one she'd seen at the bus stop that morning. Both children were eating popsicles. Coming from Kaigler's, Darby thought, hoping they wouldn't come as far as her house. The two, who looked to be about her age, kept moving closer, however, and since there was no one else in sight, it seemed rude not to be ready to speak.

Darby rose casually from the steps and walked idly to the curb. With her back to the approaching boy and girl, she held her arms out and began to curb walk.

"There's the new girl," the boy said from behind her. "I hear she's a Yankee." Darby stopped, wavering her arms for balance.

"So what?" the girl said. Darby half turned and saw that the two were almost at her yard.

"I don't like Yankees," the boy said, and he limped toward the house across the street.

"Don't pay any attention to him," the girl said, stepping toward Darby. "He thinks he's the general of the neighborhood. Just because he's had polio, everyone thinks he's as important as President Roosevelt."

Well, she'd show him that Queen of the World was above General of the Neighborhood, Darby thought, but she didn't say it. Still, she looked after the boy with interest. She'd never known anyone with polio, though everyone had been afraid of it all summer.

"My name is Valerie. He's Gordon." Valerie made a face. "He's in fifth grade. I'm in fourth. Have you been down the shoot-the-chute?"

"The what?" Darby asked.

"You mean you live next door, and you don't know about the shoot-the-chute?"

"I've only lived here three days," Darby said.

"But you can see it from your back yard. I'll show you." Valerie grabbed Darby's hand, pulling her up the sloping front yard and through the side yard. "It belongs to Jim and John, the Goodbread twins. Their father built it. They have the measles," Valerie said all in a rush.

"That's it?" Darby asked, when Valerie stopped.

Rising in the adjacent backyard like a giant wooden camel was a structure that was impossible not to see, and yet she hadn't even noticed it. Nor had Mom or Dad or Kyla or Blair. "What is it?"

"A shoot-the-chute," Valerie said, as Darby continued to stare. The structure rose and fell across most of the yard like a miniature roller coaster. Beginning from a six-foot-high platform, the track swooped down to the ground, then up a three-foot rise and down, then sharply up again to a dead-end post.

"Want to try it?" Valerie asked. Darby hesitated, eager but anxious.

"Their father built it?" she asked. In Washington they had lived next door to a man who built things—a picket fence, a bed, a lion-footed dining room table. Darby was fascinated by anyone who could take flat boards and turn them into something useful or beautiful.

"Come on," Valerie urged. "They'll let you." Again pulling Darby by the hand, Valerie ran to the Goodbreads' back door. "Have you met Darby Bannister?" Valerie began politely, introducing Darby to Mrs. Goodbread and inquiring about the boys' measles.

The next thing Darby knew, she was climbing the ladder to the platform, with Valerie instructing from below. The track came up onto the platform where there was a small flat-bed cart.

"You get on it," Valerie said, "and give yourself a little push. Hold on to the sides with your hands."

Darby sat on the cart and glanced toward her house to see if anyone was watching her go to her death.

"You're not afraid, are you?" Valerie said. "I do it all the time. We all do."

Darby was terrified, but she simply couldn't show it.

"It's fuuun," Valerie sang.

With a smile pasted on her mouth and her hands gripping the sides of the cart, Darby pulled her heel against the platform and she was off. Her tonsils shot backward through the back of her neck, and her innards sprang up through the top of her head. Eyes squeezed shut, her body rushed downward, then woosh-wooshed up and down the small rise, scrambling everything inside her. Daring to open her eyes, she saw herself propelled to a certain crash into the end post. She thought to leap free, but her hands were welded to the side of the cart.

Just before a scream could clear her throat, the flat-bed cart rolled to a stop, then reversed itself.

Swiftly, she was rolled backward to the edge of the small rise, then forward, then back, ever slowing, ever gentling until she stopped.

"How'd you like it?" Valerie shouted, pointing to the speckled faces of two look-alike boys in a window. Dazed, Darby stood by the track, her guts settling down inside of her like the fizz disappearing in a cola.

"It was fun!" she said, pleasure quickly overcoming her fear. Feeling like Queen of the Shoot-the-chute, she raised her arm and waved to the measle-y Goodbread boys.

» 6 «

» ON DARBY'S VERY FIRST DAY at school,
the boy at the desk in front of her said, "I
hope you're not like old suck-thumb Margaret."

"Who's she?" Darby asked, stricken, sliding her
left hand down onto her lap lest he see the bump
on her thumb.

"She used to sit in that desk, but she moved."

"Thank goodness," the girl next to her said.

Even though she had not sucked her thumb for
two years, there was still a knob on it from all the
years of sucking. What if they found out and
called her old suck thumb?

"Please copy the spelling words from the blackboard," Miss Hardy said. Miss Hardy was at the
blackboard writing in cursive.

The boy in front of Darby bent to his tablet. She
shifted uncomfortably in her seat. In Washington

45

she was to learn cursive this year. She glanced around and saw her classmates busy copying from the blackboard. She spotted the limping boy, Gordon, and her heart lightened at the sight of a familiar face. As he looked up at her, she smiled, but he cut off her smile by sticking out his tongue. Narrowing her eyes she mouthed the word *hateful* and turned to the board. How could she find out what the words were? One of them was *about*. She could figure that one. Another looked like *anound,* but she didn't know any such word. Tediously, she copied the words onto her tablet, smiling so that no one would guess she didn't know what she was writing.

At recess Darby saw that many of the boys and girls, including the boy who sat in front of her, were barefooted. Had he been barefooted in class? Surely she would have noticed. No, these children must have taken off their shoes for play period so as not to get them scuffed and dirty. People simply did not come to school barefooted. She watched in amazement as the barefooted ones ran and chased and did not even flinch when they scampered across the gravel driveway.

There were no organized games. Everyone just ran free, playing tag or hopscotch, or jumping rope. No one invited her to play.

Suddenly Darby saw Kyla standing alone, leaning against the building, and she ran over. No one had invited Kyla to play, either.

"Hi," she said, hurting more for Kyla than for herself. Without a word, Kyla crossed her arms and turned away from Darby.

"All right for you!" Darby said and wandered back toward the playing children. Obviously, she was not going to have a friend here, not even her sister. Hateful Gordon, she observed, seemed to be general of the schoolyard as well as the neighborhood. She made a point of ignoring him.

Refusing to look at Gordon, Darby watched the kids in line at the see-saw. She noticed that when it was their turn, each pair rode up and down ten times. Very casually, she joined the end of the line.

"Let's see-saw hard," said a barefooted girl with stick-straight hair the color of Cream of Wheat, as she mounted the see-saw opposite Darby. Darby loved a challenge.

"Okay," Darby said, thrusting her feet against the ground and sailing into the air. Her partner spread her legs wide and let the see-saw crash into the ground. Even though she was holding tightly to the handle, Darby nearly flew off the board from the unexpected jounce. So, that's the way you want to play, Darby thought. When the girl pushed up, Darby spread her own legs and let her end of the see-saw bang into the ground to return the jolt. Shocks of pain splintered through her as hard as the blows from Daddy's belt.

Next time up, Darby was prepared and enjoyed almost flying off the end. But when she landed this time, she caught with her feet before springing upward again. The ride was more fun that way. After one more bump, the girl at the other end caught with her feet, also. They completed their turn fast and flying, but without bumping. Then they dismounted, carefully avoiding speaking to each other.

Back in the building, Darby was pleased to see that the girl was in her class and sat in the same row, two seats behind. Throughout the day, Darby turned her head as if to look out the window, so she could glance back at the girl. Her see-saw friend had become her assurance that she was truly part of this fifth-grade classroom. Tomorrow there would be at least one face besides Gordon's to recognize.

»7«

WHEN DARBY DISCOVERED she was expected to write in longhand as well as read it off the blackboard, she nearly panicked. At first, she drew looping lines across the bottom of her printed letters. Without advertising it to the class, Miss Hardy corrected one or two letters on each of Darby's papers. From this, and with Mother's help, she learned that *o*'s and *v*'s and *w*'s were connected from the top of the letter, and *b*'s from the middle. The letters *f, r, s,* and *z* were the hardest to learn because they were the most different from the printed letter. Darby loved Miss Hardy for not calling attention to her deficiency. Because of this, no one in the class ever knew she was just learning cursive writing.

But Miss Hardy let everyone know about another problem of Darby's. The teacher corrected her openly whenever she forgot to use the term *ma'am,* which was all the time.

"Here in the south," Miss Hardy explained, "all well-brought-up children say *ma'am* when addressing a lady and *sir* when addressing a gentleman." Did Miss Hardy think she was not well brought up?

"We just say yes or no politely," Darby explained.

"Well, here you will say *ma'am,*" Miss Hardy said firmly.

But Darby kept forgetting. *Ma'am* would not come to her when it should. Maybe she just didn't like it. There were other expressions she knew she didn't like, too, such as *hey,* which meant "hi," and *y'all,* which meant "all of you."

At recess, she and the straw-haired girl, Fancy Potter, kept up their challenge matches. If they weren't in line to come out opposite each other, the one closest to the front let someone else get ahead. On the see-saw, they slammed their feet into the ground and pushed back up as hard and fast as possible. They did all this grim-faced and silent, but Darby was laughing on the inside. She wondered if Fancy was, too. Darby thought that she and Fancy were good secret friends.

On the way in from recess one day at the

beginning of October, John Goodbread whispered to Darby, "Your sister got put up to sixth grade."

"What? How do you know?"

"Jim said so. He's in her class. *Was* in her class. He says she was twice as smart as anyone in that whole class." Darby beamed with pleasure, overwhelmed with happiness for Kyla. Now, at last, everything would be all right, and she and Kyla would be friends again.

While Darby was still glowing from the news, a bell clanged loud and long. An air raid drill, she thought, jumping with fright. Keep calm, she told herself. That's what she had been taught to do in the air raid drills in Washington. Keep calm, and they will show you where to go and what to do. All the pupils were rising and standing by their desks, so she stood by hers as the classroom emptied, row by row. Out the door they marched, down the hall to the right, out the end door and across the school yard, until they were over near the woods.

"Where are we going?" she whispered to LeRoy, who was in front of her in class and in every line going anywhere.

"Right here. Where do you think?" he answered. He was one of the barefooted ones who did not, she had observed, put on shoes after recess. It turned out that they never wore any in the first place.

Right here, she thought? Here in the open? Suddenly she was as afraid as she would have been if it were not a drill but an actual air raid. The rumbling sound of planes rose in her ears. They would be dropping bombs, and she wouldn't have the protection of a basement or even a strong dining room table. She dropped to her knees, drew her head down into her shoulders, and covered it with her arms, as she had been taught.

"What are you doing?" LeRoy asked.

"What are *you* doing?" she asked in return, peeking up through the crook in her arm. "Is that all you do in an air raid drill? Just stand there? Don't they even tell you to kneel down and cover your head with your arms?" Arms, she had been taught, were less important than heads.

"Air raid drill? We don't have air raid drills at school. This is a fire drill, and you'd better stand up before Miss Hardy sees you."

Fire drill? Of course, a fire drill, Darby thought. Relief mixed with further anxiety. In case of fire, at least, they would be protected. But had they no plan for air raids? Standing up, she brushed the dirt from her elbows and knees. Did they think the enemy would be so courteous as to strike only when everyone was at home?

Back inside, still worried about air raids, Darby took to looking at LeRoy as well as Fancy. Because they were familiar, looking at them somehow reassured her. LeRoy, Fancy, and John Goodbread, who had recovered from the measles. She knew three people in her classroom. Gordon didn't count.

That afternoon, while she pretended to look out the window in order to glance back at Fancy, Darby saw the principal of the school breaking a branch from a flowering shrub. Their eyes met. The woman smiled and gave a tiny wave in friendly greeting, while, at the same time, warning Darby not to return the wave. The act lightened Darby's burden, and the tightness in her shoulders lessened. The day was blazingly blue, and if the principal was gathering a bouquet for the office, nothing could go too far wrong.

To Darby's surprise, the woman held the branch with one hand and, with the thumb and forefinger of the other, stripped leaf and flower from the stem. Darby cocked her head in puzzlement. The principal then began to swing the slender limb down out of Darby's sight. Unable to control her curiosity, Darby shifted in her desk, rising enough to look out. She was so startled by what she saw that she sat back down with a plop. Then, unbelieving, she half stood again to confirm the vision.

With swift strokes, the principal was striping the bare legs of a small boy. The child didn't run or cry, but stood still. Darby's eyes narrowed, and she held her throat so she would not cry out. Each blow of the switch took some of her breath away. If they called her old suck thumb and spanked her, she would never come back to this place.

"Did you see that?" she asked Fancy Potter the minute school was over.

"What?" Fancy gathered up her books and started to walk away.

"That little boy got spanked."

"He didn't get spanked; he got switched."

"So, what's the difference?" Darby stared out the window as though the spanking/switching were still going on.

"A spanking is with a hand or a belt or a paddle," Fancy said. "A switching is with a switch. The little ones and the girls get switched. The boys from the fourth up get spanked—with a paddle."

"Well, they'd better not switch me," Darby said. She didn't even get spanked at home anymore, though Dad used to really lay it on. He didn't think you'd had enough until you cried, and a year ago she'd made up her mind that she wouldn't cry even if he killed her. He decided then that she was too big for spankings. "I never heard of a teacher spanking," she said.

"I told you, it was a switching, not a spanking. And she's not a teacher, she's the principal."

"Same thing."

"Is not. The principal is the boss. Is a teacher the boss? Only of one classroom, not the whole school. Besides, she won't switch you if you behave yourself. She only switches you if you deserve it."

"Well, you don't have to sound so hateful," Darby said, wondering what the little boy had done to deserve a spanking.

"But you've ruined everything," Fancy said.

"Ruined what?" Darby said.

"We were good secret friends."

Darby laughed. "You, too?"

"Me, too, what?" Fancy said.

"I didn't know anyone did secret, silent things like I do. You were my silent friend, but I didn't know I was yours."

"Really? I thought you knew," Fancy said. "When you look at me and think about being secret friends, don't you nearly burst out laughing from trying to keep a straight face?"

"Yes," Darby said, and they let out all the laughter they'd been holding in.

"Are you and your sister twins?" Fancy asked when they'd stopped laughing.

"My sister? No, we're not twins. How do you know my sister?"

"Oh, everybody knows about your sister. They think she's the smartest person in the whole school."

"They do?" She clapped her hand over her mouth. "I have to run. I'm going to find Kyla." She left Fancy standing there and sped along the dusty pathway in front of the school.

» 8 «

» "KYLA, it's wonderful," Darby said, catching up with her sister on Stewart Avenue.

"What's wonderful?" Kyla said, sounding as dull and crabby as Gordon.

"You're in sixth grade!" Darby said. "Now everything's all right."

"Nothing's all right," Kyla snapped.

"But the whole school is talking about how smart you are!" Darby was exuberant, flapping her arms up and down and jumping around as Kyla walked.

"That doesn't make things right," Kyla said.

"Sure, things are different here," Darby said, "but this is a different place." Somehow she felt like the older sister. "In Washington we knew people because we'd lived there all our lives. Here we have to get to know people." A bus went by and Gordon, by a window, put his thumbs to his temples and waggled his fingers. Darby laughed and waved to him. He might not speak to her, but she would speak to him, anyway. Soon he'd feel ashamed of acting so snobby. "There we had streetcars, and here we have buses," she added.

"They have streetcars here, too, dumbo," Kyla said.

"Where?" Darby challenged. "Where do they have streetcars? I don't see any streetcars, and I don't see any streetcar tracks."

"Just because you don't see them doesn't mean there aren't any. You haven't seen the Eiffel Tower, but it's there just the same. It doesn't even care if you've seen it or not."

"What's the matter with you?" Darby said, putting her hands on her hips. "You're acting just as hateful as if you hadn't been put up in sixth grade."

"And you act like it matters a whole bunch. Will you just kindly shut up?"

"But we've hoped and prayed," Darby said.

"Who has?" Kyla said.

"We have. I have. Haven't you?" It was more of an exclamation than a question. "I've hoped and prayed for you to be in sixth grade where you belong."

"No place here is where I belong," Kyla said. She clutched her book satchel to her chest so firmly and glared so fiercely that Darby shut up. The hope drained from Darby like water from a bathtub when the plug doesn't fit right. She thought of Washington, which they both missed so much, and the school where they'd had such fun learning.

Here they learned mostly by sitting at their desks, listening to the teacher or reading from books or the blackboard. They left their desks only for recess, lunch, and spelling bees. In Washington, at Woodside, they'd learned in many different ways. They'd learned the days and the months and how to measure and use a ruler by making calendars. They'd learned to make change by building a grocery store, with real shelves and a counter. To stock it, they'd made clay peas and beans and papier-mâché apples and bananas, and brought empty cans and bottles from home. They'd learned about birds by observing the bird feeders they'd built and kept stocked with suet and seeds. And they'd learned about plants, soil, and growing things by planting victory gardens.

They'd done things for the war effort, too, like saving cans, string, tinfoil, and scrap rubber. They'd even made a quilt to keep a wounded soldier warm. Each of them had hemmed four squares, and they'd all helped sew the squares together. Here you wouldn't even know a war was going on, except that on Fridays everyone bought savings stamps, which were used to buy U.S. bonds.

"This school is sure different," she ventured, after they had walked the whole of Stewart Avenue in silence. "Woodside was a lot more fun."

"Damn Woodside School!" Kyla said. "It's that damn progressive school that messed everything up in the first place."

Darby reeled from the force of the words. "Mom will wash your mouth out with soap!" she said, wondering what a progressive school was, anyway.

At home, Kyla went to their bedroom and slammed the door. If Dad were home, Kyla would have to open and close the door quietly ten times, or fifty, or a hundred. He did not tolerate door slamming. Grabbing the door knob, Darby jerked it open and flung her book satchel onto the top bunk. "I have to put my things in my room, whether you like it or not," she said. "You don't own this room." Sticking out her tongue, she blew under it across her bottom lip.

"Mother! Darby's giving me the raspberry," Kyla howled.

Darby closed the door quietly and said, "Well, she deserved it," as Mother came across the hall.

Mother draped an arm around Darby's

shoulders and guided her through the kitchen to the dining room. "Maybe she does deserve it, and maybe she doesn't," Mother said, returning to the sewing machine.

"Who's that for?" Darby asked, fingering the black material and hoping it wasn't for her.

"It's my choir robe," Mother said. "I've joined the choir at church. I figure you and Kyla and Daddy can take care of Blair on choir practice nights, and on Sundays I can leave her in the nursery. She's old enough now."

"Kyla got moved up to sixth grade," Darby said casually, sitting on the floor by the sewing machine.

"I know," Mother said, guiding the cloth under the needle. "They called me."

"Why doesn't it make her happy?" Darby asked. "I was so glad when I heard it I nearly burst."

"Oh, sweetheart." Mother removed her knee from the start lever of the sewing machine and sighed. "Getting moved up doesn't erase the humiliation of having been set back in the first place."

"But nobody even knew she had been set back but the teachers. Golly, everyone thought we were twins, like Jim and John, and now I'm the dumbo because I didn't get put up."

"Kyla knew," Mother said. "And don't you start

on me." Mother lifted Darby's chin with one finger. "It's not just school. It's the moving."

"But we all moved." Darby curled her arms around her shins and rested her chin on her knees.

Mother sighed again. "Sometimes a move is harder for one person than another. Maybe it's her age."

"I'm practically the same age," Darby said. "And I don't like it, either, but I'm not sulking in my room."

"No," Mother said. "You're sulking right here in front of me so I'll be sure to know how much you suffer." They both laughed. "Try to be sweet and patient with her, okay?"

"What's a progressive school?" Darby asked.

"A progressive school tries new and different ways of making learning interesting and natural," Mother said. "Woodside was considered progressive. The schools here are traditional."

"Is it traditional for someone to get a spanking at school?"

"Uh-oh," Mother said. "What's this about spanking?" Darby told her. "Well, of course, I expect you not to get into trouble, but if any such thing happens, you tell them politely that your parents said they may not spank you. They may call me, and I'll decide what's best."

Darby pictured herself in trouble, without thinking of what the trouble might be, raising her eyebrows and chin, and saying, "My mother says you may not spank me."

"And they don't have air raid drills," Darby concluded. "The people here don't even act as though a war is going on."

"Well, Atlanta is not as vulnerable a target as Washington," Mother said.

"What's vulnerable?"

"Open to attack. Not as likely a target." Darby was thinking about Dad's being an air raid warden in Washington, walking around during an air raid drill to be sure that no neighborhood lights were visible to make a target for the enemy. "Blackouts," they were called.

"Were we in danger when we lived in Washington?" Somehow she had taken the air raid drills at home and school casually, as patriotic preparation, with no real thought that their training would be called into use. She had been more fearful on the Perkerson School grounds today than she had ever been in Washington.

"Not really. But we had more reason to be cautious," Mother said.

"Did we move because of air raids?"

"Oh, no. Your daddy was transferred."

Darby wondered. It seemed more likely that

Dad had moved his family to safety, to a less important target. If the United States could go bomb other countries, then the other countries, she thought, could come bomb the United States. Washington, D.C., she presumed, would be one of the first targets.

"Air raids are nothing to worry about," Mother said, and Darby acted satisfied, because she didn't want to talk about it anymore. But she didn't stop thinking about it. At the moment, the danger seemed very real, and that brought the whole war closer. Suddenly, Darby knew that real, live people were fighting and getting killed. It was a horrible thing to understand.

» 9 «

THE SATURDAY HABIT, Darby soon discovered, was to go to the movies. But because
of General Gordon, she was never invited. Every
Saturday at two o'clock she watched the neighborhood children traipse off. When they came
home it was worse, because they ran all over the
neighborhood, acting out the movie they'd just
seen.

"You can go, too," Valerie said one day. "I just
can't invite you to go with us. I mean, you can go
at the same time. You can even walk behind us.
It's a free sidewalk. He can't boss the sidewalk.
And if you buy your ticket, you can sit anywhere
you want. He can't stop you." At least Valerie
spoke to her. The Goodbread twins spoke only if
their mother was watching or Gordon wasn't.

"Mother doesn't let me go to movies much, anyway," Darby said, which was a mixture of truth

and falsehood. Mother never let her go to the movies with the kids in Washington. Now, however, since she was in fifth grade and also because the theater was nearby, Mother had given Darby permission to go to the movies on Saturdays. And it hurt more to have the permission than not to have it. When Mother questioned her about it, Darby shrugged and said she didn't really want to go.

"I'd stay home," Valerie said, "but it's a Hopalong Cassidy movie, and he's the best. Besides, I have to see what happens to Flash Gordon."

Darby decided to fill her Saturdays by talking to Mr. Goodbread, going to Kaigler's, and reading the Bible.

She went straight to Mr. Goodbread to talk about how things are built. "How did you make it?" she asked him about the shoot-the-chute first.

"I just cut out the pieces and put them together," he said. "Like assembling a puzzle."

"But how did you know how to cut them? How did you make the track curve? Did you have some curved boards?" He told her how he cut the curves out of flat wood, in gradual sections. He showed her how the wheels of covered wagons were made, section by section.

At Kaigler's, she spent her ten-cent weekly al-

lowance, lingering over the candy case to determine the best bargain in penny candy. Mr. Kaigler
was as gruff-sounding as ever, and she hated his
calling her *Blümchen*, especially since he knew her
name. She should, she decided, figure out some
way to check up on him, to find out if he was
really a spy.

With his wife, Mr. Kaigler lived in some room or
rooms behind the store. Today the door behind
the butcher counter was left open. "Mother asked
me to see if you had some good pork chops,"
Darby said, trying to peer beyond the pork chops
and roast beef into the living quarters. But Mr.
Kaigler, with his broad, white-aproned belly, was
quick to come to the meat case, blocking the view.

At one point, Mr. Kaigler spoke on the tele-
phone, but all he talked about was groceries. He
must have a code made up of grocery words, she
decided.

That afternoon, Darby read in the woods, sitting
with her back against the largest tree. Very quickly
she realized she could never keep up her schedule
of Bible readings. Already she was hopelessly behind. From the index she found the number of
chapters in each book and, with effort, she added
them up. One thousand, one hundred eighty-nine
chapters in the Bible. Working more arithmetic
with the number of chapters and the number of

pages, she figured out that she could read the Bible through in six months by reading only seven chapters a day, or seven-and-a-half pages a day. How much easier this was than trying to do it in two months.

Usually Darby read in order, but when she reorganized her schedule she saw that Obadiah had only one chapter. She decided that today she would read Obadiah for relief. Blessed Obadiah.

While she was reading Obadiah, Yoko came over. She hadn't seen Yoko since the day they had met, right here in these woods. She had assumed that Yoko was at the movies with the rest of the world.

"Would you like to come over to my house?" Yoko asked.

"I thought you were at the movies," Darby said. "Everyone else is."

Yoko shrugged. "They won't let me go anymore." She bobbed her head toward her house, implying it was her parents who wouldn't let her go. Darby's mind halted at the word *anymore*, which meant that Yoko used to go to the movies.

"Can you come over?" Yoko said.

"I have to read Obadiah," Darby said, deciding to be faithful to her reading.

"We can read it together," Yoko said. "We can sit in the basket swing or in the sycamore tree."

Darby looked up at Yoko with the sleek black hair and the huaraches on bare feet. This girl was making an effort to be friends, and Darby certainly wanted a friend. She looked over her shoulder at her own house. Mother wouldn't mind, as long as she was in sight of the house.

"Okay." She pushed herself to her feet and crossed Stewart Avenue with Yoko. She was soon introduced to the basket swing and the sycamore tree and the dog, Muffin. The sycamore tree, stunted years ago, had grown broad and sprawling instead of tall and straight, and Muffin could scramble up onto the broad limbs. Darby clutched at Muffin and stroked the white, shaggy fur.

"He's just the opposite of Blackie Dog," she said. "Blackie Dog was tall and black and smooth." As she cuddled the animal, he licked her face and her heart lurched. "Oh, I wish . . ." she began but stopped. Wishing for something that was hopeless was . . . well, hopeless. They had a smaller yard than before and it wasn't fenced in and Dad had made it clear that there would be no pets. She knew better than to waste her time on a for-or-against list.

Perched comfortably on the limbs of the tree, the girls passed the Bible back and forth, alternating verses as they read Obadiah aloud. " 'There is none understanding in him,' " Darby read at the end of verse seven. "And there is none much in me, either," she said, laughing.

She was surprised to see that on page 979 in her Bible, Obadiah was talking about Jacob and Esau, who were in Genesis. Obadiah was condemning Esau and his land and his people, calling them heathen. "What are the heathen?" she asked.

"The heathen are unbelievers," Yoko said, changing positions along the limb.

"Why is Esau a heathen? I don't think Esau was treated fairly," Darby said. "Or Cain, either. Why didn't God accept Cain's offering? And I hated it when Abraham was ready to sacrifice Isaac." There were so many things she didn't understand.

"You can't just take the parts you like," Yoko said. "You have to take the whole thing." The back door swung open and a man and a small child came out. "There's Daddy," Yoko said with excitement, and she started shimmying down the tree.

"No, no. Stay there," Yoko's father said. "I want to take pictures of you girls in the tree." Stooping and moving around, he held a camera in front of his face.

"Daddy's a photographer," Yoko said.

"Me, too," said the little girl, who was clutching a stuffed animal that was nearly as big as she was. "Take me, too."

"All right, Kiyo," Mr. Sasaki said, and he took the bear, handed it up to Darby, then boosted

Kiyo up to Yoko. Darby loved holding the huge, soft bear. As soon as Kiyo, who was about Blair's size, was settled, she reached out for the bear. Almost reluctantly Darby relinquished the toy. The plush black-and-white panda had been almost as good to hug as Blackie Dog.

Mr. Sasaki wandered around beneath them, calling out instructions. Darby heard a click every time he snapped a picture. Soon Mrs. Sasaki came and stood in the doorway. Darby was entranced by the beauty of this family with the sleek black hair and the golden skin. Americans, she thought with pleasure. Americans are all kinds of people.

At home, Darby looked in the dictionary for the word *heathen.* "A person who does not acknowledge the God of the Bible." Then she had to look up the word *acknowledge,* "to have knowledge of and agree to." At least she knew what that meant. Sometimes looking up a word led her all over the dictionary to other words that she didn't understand.

She went back to Genesis and reread the Jacob and Esau story, in which Jacob tricked Esau out of his birthright. It seemed that God loved Jacob the best right from the start, and she didn't understand why. How was it that God wasn't fair? God was supposed to be the most fair of all and love everyone alike, wasn't he?

"Daddy, are you a heathen?" she asked him.

"What brought that on?" he asked, and she told him. "Then I suppose I am," he said.

"David," Mother said in a warning voice, coming from the kitchen to stand in the doorway.

"If she's old enough to ask the question, she's old enough to hear my answer," he said. Mother stood stiffly in the doorway but said nothing further. Darby kept her eyes on Daddy. The air between Mother and Dad was like a tight rubber band, and she was afraid it might snap if she moved a muscle. She wished she could withdraw the question, even though she really wanted to know. But she couldn't even move enough to say, "Never mind."

"There are many ways of believing," Dad began. "Most of the people in this country believe in the Bible and the God of the Bible and in Jesus, as your mother does." He glanced at Mother. "The Jewish people believe in the Old Testament only, believing in God but not in Jesus. You remember the Solomons in Washington? They are Jewish."

Yes, Joel had been one of her friends. Of course she remembered.

"In other countries, there are holy books that people believe in just as much as some people believe in the Bible. All these people think their beliefs are the right ones," he said, "which is why I can't agree totally with any of them. They can't all be right, can they, lamb? There is good and bad in all of the teachings."

Bad, Darby thought? Bad in the Bible? Mother cleared her throat, which was the only sound she had made. Yes, bad in the Bible, like Abraham ready to sacrifice Isaac. She didn't like that kind of faithfulness. She certainly wouldn't want her mother or father to be that faithful.

"When you're older you can study the different religions for yourself," he said. "But for now, you just concentrate on what Mother can teach you about her own beliefs."

In her room, Darby climbed onto the top bunk and stared at the ceiling, brooding about heathens. Though she couldn't puzzle it out about Jacob and Esau, or about Dad, she knew that she was not a heathen. She had knowledge of and agreed to the God of the Bible. She loved God and Jesus with a whole wonder, even if there were things she didn't understand. Almost without realizing it, her arms circled the pillow as though it were her very own panda bear.

» 10 «

» MIDAFTERNOON one day at school, a strange combination of bells rang.

"Assembly," said LeRoy, turning to face Darby. It was the middle of October, and the first trace of coolness was in the air. Most of the boys and girls were now wearing shoes, but LeRoy was still barefooted. Hanging on to summer until the last, Darby thought. His feet were the same dust gray as the worn boards of the floor.

"Assembly?"

"Six weeks assembly," he said matter of factly, as he stood by his desk. By now she was thoroughly familiar with lining up and leaving the room row by row, and she was getting to know the people in her class. Fancy and LeRoy were her best school friends, but she was now friendly with a few others, as well. A good thing, too, since Gordon was still being a snob.

The boy who sat in the first desk of the first row

always led the line. When he left this time, he turned left, which was the opposite way their class went for everything else—recess, fire drills, restrooms, and lunch.

"Where are we going?" Darby whispered to LeRoy, who had just returned from a two weeks' absence, during which he'd worked on a farm picking cotton. Darby had been wide-eyed with envy at the thought of such adventure.

"To the auditorium," he said. She frowned and pointed to the right, toward the lunchroom, as she followed the line to the left. Didn't they have assembly in the lunchroom? In her old school, there was one large room in which tables were set up for lunch, and chairs were set up for assemblies. It was also the place where they played indoor games and had dancing and acrobatics.

As the line continued down the hall, Darby became uneasy. At the very center of the building, both front and back, were broad, windowed doors which spilled light across the hallway. Darby had never before been farther than those doors. Now she was well past them. The floor seemed to tilt, and the walls moved toward her, closing her in.

She tried to convince herself that these floors and walls were just like the ones at the other end of the hall, the comfortable, secure end. Vaguely she remembered that the kindergarten through

third-grade classrooms were at this end of the
school. But it seemed as though the little ones
were not even there. In spite of her efforts to be
reasonable, Darby shrank from this alien territory.

For reassurance she looked for her friends.
There was LeRoy ahead of her, but it wasn't
LeRoy at all—it was some raggedy, dirty-footed
country boy. Looking behind her, her eyes sought
Fancy, but the one girl with whitish-blonde hair
didn't seem to be Fancy. Behind her, she could see
the path of daylight falling across the floor from
the windows in the familiar entrance doors.

"Run," something wild and frightened cried out
from within her. But, just like the time when she
wanted to leap from the shoot-the-chute and
couldn't, her feet were somehow locked onto the
track that was taking all the other feet down the
hall.

The auditorium was a huge, gulping space,
large enough to swallow them all. What was wrong
with her? In Washington she had always enjoyed
new places. Here, each new place she went frightened her.

LeRoy sat in the last seat on one row. Instead of
starting down the next row, alone and in the lead,
Darby tried to squeeze in next to LeRoy. Fussing
and shoving started behind her.

"Go on, Darby," a voice said. The girl behind

her pushed, and she finally understood that she must go down the next row. When she came to the aisle she sat automatically. The child-beater principal stood on the stage. She was saying something, but Darby couldn't understand the words or make the face look familiar, even though she knew whose it was.

"It's just the principal," she told herself, but she wasn't comforted. Singing began, and the strangeness increased because she had never heard the songs before. Some strange words about a boll weavil and a Swannee River.

During the third song, she was sitting miserably with her hands on her lap when the girl next to her, the one who had pushed, nudged her.

"Sing," the girl said.

"I don't know it," Darby murmured.

"Of course you do." The girl was clapping hands in time with the music. "It's 'Jimmy Crack Corn,' the one we dance to."

"Jimmy Crack Corn"? Was it "Jimmy crack corn and I don't care"? Darby listened and slowly the song became familiar. "Jimmy Crack Corn," she said to herself, smiling a little. I know that song. She began to sing, " 'Jimmy crack corn and I don't care, my master's gone away.' " She clapped her hands, and her mind eased a little more.

When the song was over, the strangeness rushed

back for a moment. But the next song was "God Bless America," and she knew that one, too. She smiled as she sang, looking around at all her classmates singing. The next song was "America the Beautiful," and she knew it, too. The auditorium began to shrink in size, and she saw Fancy two seats away from her and LeRoy at the end of the row in front of her. Miss Hardy was at the door.

Sighing with relief, she sang happily and looked around the small auditorium. She even spotted Kyla over on the other side with the sixth graders, and Valerie with the fourth graders. This is just school, she thought. Just Perkerson School. There is no cause to be afraid.

❖» 11 «❖

❖» AFTER SCHOOL, Darby wanted to talk and be friends with everyone, to express her sure feelings of familiarity. Even the classmates she didn't know were no longer threatening. They would never call her old suck thumb.

Walking away from school with Fancy, she discovered that they went the same way at the corner. Suddenly Fancy ran ahead a few steps, stomped her foot on the ground, twirled three times, and said, "My luck."

"What's that for?" Darby asked, looking to see if Fancy had found a penny.

"A Lucky Strike," Fancy said. "If you step on it first and turn three times, it's your luck."

"How can you tell if it's a Lucky Strike?" Darby asked, looking along the ground as she walked. She saw several cigarette butts but had no idea how to tell whether they were Lucky Strikes or not.

"It's written on it, silly," Fancy said. Darby picked up a cigarette butt to look, but Fancy knocked it out of her hand.

"Don't pick that up," Fancy said. "It's filthy."

"Well, how can I find out what kind it is?" Darby asked. She was beginning to think that Fancy didn't want her to have any luck. Maybe Fancy didn't want to be friends, after all.

"It's the package, Darby. The package!" Fancy burst out laughing and ran back and picked up the package between her thumb and forefinger. The white package had a large red circle with the words "Lucky Strike" lettered in black. Darby walked with her eyes to the ground partly because she was looking for Lucky Strikes and partly because she felt like such a dumbo again.

When Fancy started to cross the street partway down Stewart, Darby moved across the street, too. "How far do you live?" she asked. "I thought maybe I could come by your house for a minute to see where you live."

"Won't your mother be mad?" Fancy said, pausing at the opposite curb.

"Not if I hurry," Darby said, stepping onto the curb herself and leading the way as if she knew it. "If I don't stay long and if I run when I leave."

"Well, I—I have work to do and—"

"Just for a minute. Just to see where you live. Then one day maybe you can come home with me."

Fancy shook her head. "My mama and papa believe in us staying home."

But Darby was persistent. She started down the slope ahead of Fancy. "They won't mind me coming, will they?"

Fancy shrugged. "My daddy don't like city people much."

"I'm not city people," Darby said. "I'm county people. Besides, I'll just stay a minute. I won't even come in. They won't hardly know I'm there."

Weeds brushed their legs as they descended the path down the slope. In five steps they had totally disappeared from the road above them.

"Hey, this is nifty," Darby said.

"What's nifty?" Fancy asked, making her way down the hill.

"Being right here next to the road but not being able to see it," Darby said.

Below them was a tiny, loose-boarded, unpainted house. "Oh, a playhouse," Darby said. Fancy didn't respond.

Behind and to the side of the playhouse was the skeleton of a house being built. Hammer blows rang through the air. In the dirt yard of the playhouse, two barefooted little boys played. The younger one was bare-bottomed as well.

"Hey, Fancy," the little boys said when they saw the girls. "You better be glad you're here. Papa's been wanting water." Darby looked from the boys to the little house. A movement had caught her eye, and she saw a woman in the doorway, behind the dark screen.

"Hey, Fancy, there. Draw me a bucket," a deep voice called from across the yard. Darby looked over at the new house and saw a man in work overalls with a hammer in his hand.

"Coming, Papa," Fancy called. She set her books in the dust and walked away.

Darby's heart leaped. "Is that your father?" she asked with a bit of awe.

"Uh-huh."

"Can he build a house?" Darby followed along behind Fancy.

"I reckon so. He's doing it." Fancy approached a tiny square wall with a roof above it. Fascinated, Darby watched while Fancy lifted a bucket from the ledge, dropped it, and began speedily unwinding a handle, which let out rope from a reel and lowered the bucket.

"What are you doing?" Darby asked.

"Getting water. What do you think?"

Darby raised herself to the ledge and looked over. "I don't see any water."

"It's down there. Just listen. You'll hear the bucket slap the water in a minute." Darby watched the bucket until it disappeared and splashed in the darkness.

"How do you get it filled?" she asked. If the bucket hit the water right side up, how could Fancy get water in it?

"Don't you know anything?"

"I never saw a well before." The song about the old oaken bucket was all she knew about wells, and this bucket was metal.

"Nothing much to them," Fancy said, as she began rewinding the handle. "Just a hole filled with water."

"How do you know the bucket has water in it?" Darby asked.

Fancy frowned and looked disgusted. "Here. Hold this. Mind, it's heavy," she warned. Darby followed Fancy's instructions and put her hand alongside Fancy's on the handle. It wasn't so heavy. Then Fancy let go. The handle jerked out of Darby's hand and spun like a whirlwind. Darby drew her hand back quickly. With a crashing splash the bucket hit the water.

"What happened?" Darby cried out.

Looking more disgusted than ever, Fancy sagged her shoulders.

"Fancy, what's takin' you so long?" her father bellowed. "My throat's cracking like a sun-baked mud flat, and you're fooling around."

"You let the bucket fall," Fancy said. "You got me in trouble." Fancy began winding again.

Darby pulled her shoulders and arms in close to her side. "I got you in trouble?"

"You let the bucket fall."

"It was heavy."

Fancy's mouth dropped open. "Of course it was heavy. It had water in it. I told you it was heavy. Are you stupid or something?"

"Let me wind it. I won't drop it again."

"I can't. He'll whip my tail if I don't hurry."

"Fancyyy!" her father bellowed again.

The rope wound around the stem of the handle in even rows until the bucket, brimming with water, rose to the top. Fancy eased the bucket onto the ledge, transferred the water to another bucket, and set out across the yard.

"You better not come," Fancy said to Darby as Darby began to follow.

"Hey, you in trouble for playing around," the older of the two boys said as he played, making roads in the dirt with a small scrap of wood from the new house.

"I'll just go now," said Darby, suddenly feeling unwelcome. She shifted her weight from one foot to the other and swung her arms aimlessly, sort of waiting for Fancy to encourage her to stay. Fancy was now six feet away and did not turn back to speak or look. "I'll run on along and I'll see you tomorrow," Darby said. She picked up her books from the ground and backed away toward the road. The little boys played happily in the dirt, and the woman watched from behind the screen door of the playhouse.

She'd felt so good at school. What had gone wrong so quickly? It was more than letting the bucket drop, but she didn't know what. Was it that Fancy had gotten all the luck from the Lucky Strike packages, and she hadn't gotten any? She wanted to draw water from the well to prove to Fancy that she wouldn't drop it. And she wanted to know how the bucket filled. Most of all, she wanted to go over by the new house and watch Mr. Potter build.

All the way home on Stewart Avenue, Darby searched diligently for Lucky Strike packages. She didn't find one.

» 12 «

>> AFTER THAT DAY, Fancy stopped see-saw-ing at recess. Forlorn, but trying not to show it, Darby still stood in the see-saw line, riding with whomever wound up opposite her. While she moved up and down automatically, her eyes roved the schoolyard, searching for the whitish-blonde straw-straight hair.

Walking home from school, Darby scuffed her way up the street. She saw that the neighborhood kids had gathered, like a mocking club, in the street between her house and Valerie's and Gordon's.

It was a few days before Halloween, and they had been making pumpkins and witches and cats at school. Miss Hardy had showed them how to make a jumping cat by folding strips of paper like an accordian, in order to construct springy arms and legs. Darby had made hers orange and black and named it Fidget. She was bouncing him as she walked along, pretending to be so engrossed as to not even see Gordon and his bunch when she passed.

"I've been through so much that I'm not afraid of anything anymore," Gordon was saying loudly, for Darby to hear. "I'll even stand under the trestle on Halloween night."

"Oh, sure, I really believe that," said Sonny, one of the other boys in the neighborhood, the tallest one. He was older than Gordon, but he followed Gordon.

"Sure I will. I don't believe in ghosts, anyhow." He clearly wanted Darby to hear, because he kept talking loudly. She slowed her step, dancing Fidget in the air, still acting absorbed in her own actions.

"From what I hear, you'd better believe in this ghost," Sonny said. "You know Mr. Williams, with the white hair? They say it turned white overnight, after he'd stood under the trestle to prove there was no ghost."

"Yeah, well, I don't believe it," Gordon said, "and I'm going to do it Halloween night. I'll bet she won't do it." He snapped his head in Darby's direction.

"What ghost? What trestle? Sure I'll do it," she

said, raising her head with interest but not speed-
ing her step. He was challenging her, but it was
the first move he'd made toward her, the first ac-
knowledgment that she even existed. If she was
going to show him that she was Queen of the
World, she'd have to accept the challenge.

"Tell her about the trestle," Gordon instructed
Valerie.

"Yes, tell me about the trestle," Darby said, turning to Valerie and ignoring the fact that he could
easily have told her himself.

"Well, you know the trestle up on Stewart, past
the drugstore?"

"No," she said. She knew the drugstore. It was
on the corner two blocks into the city. "Do you
pass it on the way to the library?" She'd been to
the library, but she hadn't noticed any trestle.

"Yes. You go right under it. Well, anyway, they
say . . ." Valerie paused, trying to sound mysteri-
ous. "They say that a long time ago a woman was
killed by a train while she was walking across the
trestle. And at night, any night, but especially on
Halloween, she screams out, warning people not
to walk the trestle. They call her the Lady of the
Trestle. A few years ago Mr. Williams went down
there to prove there was no such thing, and his
hair turned white overnight."

"I don't believe any of it," Gordon said.

"I don't think you'd look good with white hair, Gordon," Jim Goodbread said.

"I dare any of you scaredy cats to go down there with me Halloween night. I'll stand under that trestle for fifteen minutes." He carefully avoided looking at Darby, but she felt that his words were directed at her in particular. Shutting her out wasn't enough for him. He wanted to conquer her, too.

"I'll go," Darby said. If he thought she was afraid of him, or thought she couldn't do something he could do, then she would have to show him he was wrong. She would show him that she was Queen of the World.

"Okay," he said. "Nine o'clock on Halloween night."

The day before Halloween was Saturday. Darby decided that while they were at the crummy old movie, she would walk down and take a look at the trestle.

"I'm going for a walk," she told her parents. "Maybe to the drugstore." Since they believed mightily in fresh air and leg power, they said okay. If she walked under the trestle in the daylight, she reasoned, she would take some of the fear out of it.

At the drugstore she looked in the windows. A cardboard penguin with an animated flipper was lifting an unlit cigarette to its beak and blowing endless smoke rings. Darby wondered where the smoke came from. Behind the penguin, which was an advertisement for the cigarettes it smoked, the wall clock showed two o'clock.

Moving down Stewart along the tall unwindowed sides of the drugstore building, she was out of her territory again, on unfamiliar ground. The only times she'd come by this way, she was on the bus going to the library or, with Mother, to town.

The sidewalk was squeezed between the brick wall of the drugstore and the street. There was no grassy strip next to the street. Usually, Darby looked for four-leafed clovers along those strips, and it would be good to have one now. Also, when a car whizzed by, the sidewalk seemed too narrow and the building threatened to crush her.

Just beyond the drugstore building was a scrubby vacant lot. There was no clover, but at least there was open space. Directly ahead was the trestle, dark and forbidding even in the daylight. Suddenly she spotted a round, red circle at the edge of the lot. A Lucky Strike package! She stomped her foot on it, twirled three times, and said "My luck" out loud. Feeling much safer, she went on.

"It's just a bridge," she told herself as she approached the trestle. "And not even a big bridge." Just long enough to span the street, the structure was only wide enough to accommodate one set of tracks. The open network of tracks and crossties formed crisscross stripes of shadows, between which the sun came through. As she walked under the trestle, the sunlight patched her like a turtle shell.

Just one track, she thought suddenly. How do the engineers know when a train is coming from the other direction? Would two trains come along now, at the same time, and have a fiery crash above her? Would she be able to run away fast enough, before the debris fell on her? As though it were really happening, she darted out from under the track and into the full sunlight. At the rear of the drugstore, she stood and looked back at the trestle, watching freight cars and passenger cars collide, buckle, and tumble in a mass across Stewart Avenue.

"Kyla is right," she said to herself. "You are a dumbo! A dumbo and a scaredy cat."

Resolutely, she marched back under the trestle.

"Are you really there, Lady of the Trestle?" she said aloud. "Are you really there?" She looked up through the tracks and onto the concrete abutments that shouldered the bridge. "You won't frighten me, will you, Lady of the Trestle? Not today and not on Halloween or anytime." She stood very still, in case there was an answer. "I really am sorry about what happened to you," she continued. "I think it is very good of you to warn people not to cross the trestle. I'll bet you don't even bother people walking under, do you?"

For a long time she stood, listening for the Lady of the Trestle. If there was a chance that the Lady might answer and give her reassurance, she wanted to hear it. Finally, she walked slowly back to the drugstore and peeped through the glass. Ten after two. Only ten minutes? Had she had all that fright in only ten minutes? How would she stay there for fifteen minutes in the dark? Should she go back now and stay longer just for practice? Her parents might worry if she stayed away too long, she thought. Relieved, she headed back to the safety of Athens Avenue.

Borrowing her mother's Bible because it had an alphabetical index of many of the things in the Bible, she looked up *fear*. Its first appearance was in Genesis 15:1. God was speaking to Abram, whom he later called Abraham, in a vision. "Fear not, Abram," God said, "I am thy shield and thy exceeding great reward."

Darby smiled and lay back on her bed, with the

Bible open across her chest. She could hear God's great booming voice, saying, "Fear not, Darby Bannister. I am thy shield and thy great reward." He is my shield, she thought. If the Lady of the Trestle had not spoken to her and given her reassurance, God had, and that was better. Darby felt herself filling with strength and bravery and happiness, until she could hardly stand it and had to read some more.

The next passage with *fear* was in the middle of the Abraham and Isaac story, just when God stopped Abraham from killing Isaac. God was saying that He knew Abraham feared God, because he had not withheld Isaac. Darby quickly turned back to the Bible index. She hated that story about Isaac and didn't like to think about a God who would require such a thing. The first time she read it, she had tried to picture herself trusting God so much that she would prepare to sacrifice her own child, but she knew she would never do it. There must be something about the story she didn't understand, just as there was something about Yankees and rebels she didn't understand.

Next came a verse with *fear* that she didn't understand at all. Then there was one out of the Joseph and the Pharoah story, in which Joseph said, "I fear God." Darby skipped past that, too.

There was a lot of talk in the Bible about fearing God, and Darby didn't understand that, either. How could God be loving and fearsome at the same time? She felt friendly and comfortable with God, and she certainly wasn't afraid of Him. She returned to the first scripture she'd looked up and let Him be her shield and her great reward.

» 13 «

"WHAT HAVE YOU GOT TODAY?" her
teammates at Sunday school asked. It was
Halloween, though nobody mentioned it, to
Darby's surprise. She knew that Halloween was
short for All Hallow E'en and Hallow meant holy.
So, she thought, Halloween should be a special
event in Sunday school.

"Forty-nine more chapters and seven memory
verses," she said, pleased that they were interested.
Sticking doggedly to her schedule of seven
chapters a day, she was now plowing her way
through First Chronicles and the long lists of the
begats. She was memorizing a verse from each
day's readings and naming her own children as
she read. She would have twelve children, she decided, and name them all from the Bible. Some of

95

the Bible names rolled smoothly on her tongue. Hananiah, Kishi, Micah, Jabex, Malachi.

"When are you going to do something else, like bring a visitor?" someone asked. "We get points for that, too, you know."

"A visitor?" she said, offended, thinking she was already doing enough. But she would like to bring a visitor. It would prove she had a friend. Certainly none of her Sunday school classmates had become her friend, though the ones on her team liked her points well enough.

One of the boys suddenly shouted and waved an envelope above his head. "We have a letter. We have a letter," he said.

"Shhh. He has a letter."

"So what. It doesn't count in the contest."

The superintendent got them quiet. "Here's another letter for the Boys' Bataan Prayer Band."

"The what?" Darby whispered to the girl next to her.

"The prayer band."

"The what kind of prayer band?" Darby asked and was shushed from all sides. The boy was reading the letter, while Darby was trying to decipher the word that had been said just before *prayer band*. Was it *baton*? Did they play instruments and parade around while they prayed? By the time she was ready to listen, the letter was over.

"Signed, Lieutenant General James H. Doolittle," the boy read.

General Doolittle! Darby's attention was suddenly riveted. "How did he get a letter from General Doolittle?" No one shushed her this time because no one heard her. They were too busy clapping.

"The prayer band wrote to him," someone said when she repeated her question.

"Is that what they do? Write letters?"

"And pray."

"I get it," she said. "They band together to write letters and pray. Right?" She was full of questions as assembly adjourned and she went to her classroom, the familiar place with the yellow chair shawls.

Her teacher told her about the Boys' Bataan Prayer Band, which prayed for the soldiers at war. Bataan was a place in the Phillipines where the United States had lost an important battle and thousands of soldiers had been captured. One of the boys' classes had started the prayer band a year ago. They had written to the allied commander and told him of the prayer group. Later, the group had received letters and autographed pictures from some of the famous generals, as well as one from President Roosevelt himself.

The minute class was over, Darby popped out

the door and ran to the boys' class to see the pictures. She entered the room as though it were a shrine. On the wall she recognized pictures of Generals Eisenhower, MacArthur, and Patton. There were others she didn't recognize.

"I want to join the prayer band," she said to the teacher of that class, as he stood in the doorway, saying good-bye to his boys.

"I'm glad you're interested," he said, touching the last boy on the head, "but this is a special thing that our class is doing."

"Couldn't it be the Boys' and Girls' Bataan Prayer Band and be for everyone?" she asked. She knew, of course, that she could pray for the generals herself. But she thought it was more important to do something with other people. Especially since the war seemed so remote here in Atlanta, when it had been so central in Washington. Here, the only time she had any sense of the war was on Fridays, when almost everyone but Fancy and LeRoy brought a dime for savings stamps. Except when, at home, they made balls of string and tinfoil and cut both ends out of cans and stomped them flat.

"This is just for our class," the teacher said. "Your class can do something special, too. Why don't you have a prayer group for the nurses?" He looked so tall, standing there in the frame of the door, his head almost touching the top.

"Sir?" she said, looking way up. How could anyone reject her offer of prayers? He excused himself and walked away. Nurses? Of course, nurses needed prayers, too, but she didn't know any nurses, except for Florence Nightingale, who was not in this war. It was the soldiers she wanted to pray for. She'd show them. She would write to the generals herself.

At home after dinner she approached Kyla. "May I please borrow some of your writing paper?" Kyla was forever writing letters to friends "back home" in Washington.

"No," Kyla said, predictably.

"It's for something important," Darby said. If she wasn't going to be in the Boys' Bataan Prayer Band, she would do it quietly, privately. Prayer wasn't something she should brag about.

"What important could you possibly have to write?" Kyla said. "In all these weeks you haven't written to your friends once."

Darby shrugged. She had thought of them—Joyce, Bernie, Mary, Joel—but she had not written to them, nor had they to her, even though she had sworn and they had sworn. Darby stuck out her tongue and made a raspberry. She regretted it immediately. She shouldn't act unholy when she was trying to do something holy, even if Kyla was being mean.

"Here's some writing paper," Mother said, opening the secretary and holding out two boxes of stationery. One had red roses on white paper and the other was plain pale gray. She liked the roses, but the plain paper looked solemn and serious, so she chose it.

"How many sheets do you want?" Mother asked, her fingers lifting one. Darby shrugged. How many generals were there? MacArthur, Patton, Eisenhower, Doolittle. And, of course, President Roosevelt. She hated to say "Five." Mother would be too curious about what she was doing.

"May I please take the box and use what I need? I won't waste any." Mother handed over the box, telling her that the envelopes were underneath. And what about stamps? Oh, surely Mother would give her stamps.

She sat down at the dining room table. You can pray for the generals without writing to them, she told herself. Still, what she really wanted was letters back. How special it would be, what a Queen-of-the-World feeling, to have letters from the generals.

She picked up her pencil, then decided that

pencil was too childish. She opened her mouth to ask Kyla for a pen and thought better of it. She turned to her mother instead. "Mother, could I borrow your pen if I'm real careful?"

Mother sighed. "Oh, Darby, you'll just make a mess."

"I'll be real careful. Please. It's important."

Mother handed her the pen and took the cap off. "You hold it this way, and just write lightly. If you press down too hard, you'll ruin the point." Mother patted Darby's cheek.

Darby leaned over the paper. She couldn't decide which letter to write first, so decided to do them in alphabetical order. General James Doolittle. "Dear General Doolittle," she began, forming her letters just as carefully as possible. On the second sentence, ink dripped out onto the paper. She began again, but with all her care she kept making ink blobs. There was ink all over her index and middle fingers as well. It's because it's Halloween, she decided. The witches are against me.

She washed her hands and wiped the pen with toilet paper. Then she returned the pen to Mother and the box of stationery to the desk drawer. "Thank you," she said to Mother.

"Are you through?"

"Yes," she said. And for that lie she would have

to invent other reasons for wanting more stationery later, or save up her allowance to buy some of her own, which would take weeks. Kyla had bought writing paper at the drugstore for forty-nine cents. In disgust, she took her Bible and went to the woods to read.

❖» 14 «❖

❖» VALERIE CAME to the door at suppertime. "Are you going trick or treating with us?" she asked.

"Trick or treating? What's that?" Darby asked.

"You don't know what trick or treat is?" Valerie asked.

Turning toward her parents at the dining room table, Darby said, "Can I go trick or treating with Valerie and the others?" Whatever it was, it was the first time she'd been invited to do anything with them. The trestle was not an invitation but a challenge.

"Oh, sweetheart, I don't think so," Mother said.

"No, I don't think so," Dad confirmed.

"Why not?" she said. Her voice came out in a whine, which she quickly shook out of her words. Dad didn't give permission for anything to a whiner. Then she thought of a clever remark that he often made to anyone who said, "I think so." She signaled Valerie to wait a minute and ran to the dining room. "Do you think so or know so?" She smiled and used all her charm.

"I know so, sweetheart."

She started to beg and plead, but then she decided that whatever trick or treating was, it wasn't as important as going to the trestle at nine o'clock. "Well, I'm going with them later when they go to the trestle, okay?" She ran back to the door and told Valerie she'd meet them on the corner at a quarter to nine.

In Washington, someone usually had a Halloween party. It hadn't occurred to her until just this minute that she might have asked to have one. The side porch would have been a good place, too. Her imagination started soaring, as she thought of decorations she might have made. Then she shrugged. Who would she have invited? Just Yoko.

"What's this trestle business?" Dad asked when she returned to the table. "What's this later business? It's already getting dark."

She explained it to him, eagerly but reasonably. He was, at least, a person she could discuss things with. The dark wouldn't bother him. He was the one who told her she wouldn't melt in the rain or disappear in the dark. She was sure he would see the importance, after all this time of not having friends, of going with the others and proving that she was brave.

"Brave has nothing to do with it," he said. "That's several blocks from home and too late for you to be out."

"But—"

"No buts about it, little lady," he said. "I'm sorry, lamb. I know it's important for you to make friends, and I know Gordon has been making it hard for you, but we're not letting you go traipsing down to the trestle at nine o'clock at night."

"But there's no real ghost," she said. "It's just a challenge."

He reached out to where she sat at his left and ruffled her short hair. "I know there's no real ghost, sweetheart, but that's just too far from home to be after dark."

"Then why can't I go trick or treating?" She had been ready to trade one for the other, and now it looked as though she wouldn't have either.

"Do you know what it is?" Mother asked.

Darby wished for something clever to say, but could think of nothing.

"It's begging," Kyla said. "Begging and bribery."

"The children go knock on people's doors," said Mother, "and when someone comes to the door they say 'Trick or treat.' And if they don't get a treat, they play a trick."

The idea horrified Darby. "What kind of treat? What kind of trick?"

"Oh, candy, popcorn, an apple."

"And people give it?"

"Usually. Or else they'll have a pin stuck in their doorbell, or something."

Darby puzzled over the pin in the doorbell, until Daddy explained that it was to hold the button in and make it keep on ringing. "It sounds like fun," she said, imagining herself loaded down with all kinds of good things to eat.

"Oh, no," Mother said. "It's threats. Bribes, like Kyla said. Your father and I don't approve of it."

What did Kyla care, anyway? She didn't want permission to go anywhere or do anything. Kyla had never even ridden on the Goodbreads' shoot-the-chute. Darby let her shoulders sag.

Later, she watched from the window as costumed children moved up and down the street. Some came to their house. Even though Mother and Dad wouldn't let her go out and do it, they let Blair give candy corn to the ones who came here. That's not right, Darby thought. If you don't believe in it, you shouldn't give out treats. But she didn't say it.

At seven-thirty, she belly-flopped on the floor to

listen to the radio. Kyla assumed an identical position beside her, and Mom and Dad sat in chairs on either side of the radio. Every Sunday night they listened to "Inner Sanctum Mysteries." The show began and ended with the sound of an eerie squeaking door. Darby stared at the radio as though it were movies, looking through and beyond the radio, envisioning the action somewhere between her head and the space beyond. She was sorry when it was over. For a few minutes she had forgotten the real world and the kids outside, who, after nearly two months, had finally given her a chance to be friends—a chance she'd had to lose.

Miserable, she stood in the shadows of the side porch and watched the kids gather on the corner. Gordon, Valerie, Jim and John Goodbread, and Sonny were there. The group stood waiting, looking at her house for a while. Then they moved on up Athens Avenue without her.

» 15 «

» IN THE MORNING, BEFORE SCHOOL, Darby zipped around to Kaigler's for a quart of milk. Running around the corner, she almost bumped into Mr. Kaigler.

"Oh," she said with surprise and a little fright. For a split second she thought he knew she was spying, had seen her coming, and had purposely planned to scare her. Then she saw that he was washing the windows in front of the store.

"Eh, *Blümchen,* thanks for the free soap," he said, pushing a long-handled wiper up and down the window.

"Free soap?" she asked. She hadn't given him any soap. What was he talking about? If he wasn't a spy, he was at least crazy, she decided.

"The soap. The soap," he said, flapping his arms and pointing to the windows. "Saves me the price."

Darby looked bewildered. "Ah, I see, you didn't have a thing to do with it. I thought not. You're a nice girl. I should have known a nice girl like you wouldn't soap an old man's windows. Hah. A Halloween prank. Some prank." He went back to scrubbing the windows and Darby, still puzzled, pushed through the door and into the store.

"A quart of milk, please," she said to Mrs. Kaigler, who was seldom in the store.

"They don't know what work it causes," the woman said, as she took a quart of milk from the cooler. "Or maybe they do. Look at that. Just look at that. It's dark enough in here without soapy windows."

Mrs. Kaigler set the bottle of milk on the counter, as Darby turned to look out the window. The soap film on the window did block out the light. But hadn't Mr. Kaigler done it on purpose, to clean the windows? Or was it a Halloween trick some kids had played? Had they expected a storekeeper to give them a treat?

Darby set the money on the counter and picked up the cold milk. She hugged it to her side.

When she left, to make sure Mr. Kaigler knew she had had nothing to do with his windows being soaped, she said, "I'd help you, but I have to go to school."

"Right, *Blümchen*. Go to school. Go to school.

Here's hoping some other people go to school, too. Maybe they learn something. Like not to soap people's windows." She left him grumbling to himself and went home for breakfast.

By the time she was ready for school, spies and soaped windows were forgotten. With great excitement she responded to the sounds of children on the street, and ran out to hear all about last night's trip to the trestle. At least they were ready to include her in things, if only in a challenge.

"Hi," she said to Valerie as she approached the street.

"Hey," Valerie said.

"Tell her she's a coward," Gordon said, spitting the words at her via Valerie. "She was too scared to go to the trestle." Valerie looked at Darby and shrugged.

"My daddy wouldn't let me," she said, speaking directly to Gordon rather than channeling her words through Valerie.

"Daddy wouldn't let me, Daddy wouldn't let me," Gordon mocked in a sing-song voice.

"Well, he wouldn't," she began. She was going to explain how much she really wanted to go and that she wouldn't have been afraid, but he interrupted with another explosion of words.

"Coward, scaredy-cat, chicken yellow," he said. Then, realizing that he'd spoken to her directly, he repeated to Valerie. "Tell her she's a coward, scaredy-cat, and chicken yellow." The Goodbread twins looked on in admiration at his onslaught. To please his audience, Gordon started dancing around her, repeating the words, pelting her with them.

All in one great burst, Darby's anger exploded. She flew at him, fighting, not minding that Dad hated fighting, not minding that Gordon had had polio. She pummeled his chest and arms, grabbed his shirt front, and kicked his shins. Her attack surprised him so that she got in a few solid blows before he hit back.

Shouting "Coward, scaredy cat, chicken-yellow, yellow Jap lover!" he punched and grabbed at her in return. Valerie screamed and danced around them, darting out a tentative hand, trying and failing to find the courage to reach in and break them up. Suddenly Dad was there, grabbing Darby by the collar, grabbing Gordon by the collar, and holding them away from each other at arm's length.

"She hit me first," Gordon said.

"He called me names," Darby said. Dad let Gordon loose but put his arm firmly around Darby and shepherded her to the house. She turned and glared once at Gordon, who was glaring back.

"Now what was that all about?" Dad said when

they were inside. Hot stinging tears burned at the back of her eyes, but she would not let them out. She would not cry. She would not.

"He thinks I'm a coward because I didn't go to the trestle last night," she said. "I told him you wouldn't let me go, but he kept calling me scaredy cat and coward and yellow."

"If you're going to fight every time someone says something you don't like, you're going to waste a lot of time fighting, lamb."

"And Jap lover. He called me a Jap lover." She stomped her foot. "Why would he say that? I save string and tinfoil and buy savings stamps on Fridays. I'll bet he doesn't even save tinfoil! Why would he call me a Jap lover?"

In fact, she was a Jap hater. Weren't they at war with Japan? Once a neighbor in Washington had stood on the sidewalk and invited them all to join in smashing a whole collection of demitasse cups and saucers because they were made in Japan. Darby had broken her share, and what a pleasure it had been, as though she'd been smashing the Japanese themselves against the sidewalk. How dare he call her a Jap lover?

"Because of your friend Yoko, I guess," Dad said.

"Yoko? What does Yoko have to do with it?"

"Because she's Japanese," he said, holding his

large hands lightly against the sides of her face. "Of Japanese heritage, that is."

Japanese? The word hit her like thunder and she understood everything—Gordon's words, Yoko's reluctance to give in to questioning about where she was from besides Atlanta. Japanese! "But she was born here!" Darby said, trying to deny it.

"Of course she was. She's as American as you are, but because her heritage is Japanese and we are at war with Japan, some ignorant people act as though she's an enemy."

Does that make me ignorant, Darby wondered? Because she suddenly felt as though Yoko was an enemy, and she was all hollow inside. Her one friend, her only friend. Another spy. The word grew large inside her head.

» 16 «

YOKO WAS JAPANESE. Yoko was now an enemy. Darby looked out from her bedroom window and stared across the narrow woods at Yoko's white house. Sometimes she saw Yoko come onto the porch and disappear into the basket swing and she was sad, sad about wars and enemies. She sat rubbing the soft rabbit's foot and thinking of something large and cuddly, like a panda bear. She would ask for one for Christmas.

How could the war, which had seemed as remote here as the Saturday movies the others attended, touch her so closely? The people here were so little involved in the war. When the occasional convoy drove by, the children didn't line the streets, waving to and saluting the soldiers as they did in Washington. And yet here her life had been invaded by Japanese, by Germans, by spies.

114

Her resolve to spy on Mr. Kaigler increased. She would watch and gather evidence and become a hero for exposing him. But with trying to save her allowance for writing paper, she had no money to spend at Kaigler's.

In order to spy, she worked out a routine of playing in the woods every day after school and of walking the sidewalk along Deckner beside Kaigler's. These daily rituals would become so ordinary that no one would notice.

With a stone, she drew a hopscotch on the sidewalk beside the brick wall of Kaigler's store. Using two markers, she took turns with herself. From time to time, she stopped playing to examine the bricks for signs of a secret passage or a place to hide coded messages. There were no windows on this side of the store, just the solid wall, so the Kaiglers couldn't see her unless they came outside.

Her first observation was that someone else had a daily ritual, too. Every day a man she had never seen before walked a huge white dog. The dog was like a fluffy German shepherd with a curly tail. He walked across from the sidewalk, along the fringe of woods. Even after the dog had relieved itself, the man kept walking back and forth, back and forth. Was he an FBI man walking the dog for cover? He couldn't very well sneak around with a dog like that. Maybe he was doing the same thing she was doing, being so obvious that no one would be suspicious. Should she ask? He wouldn't, of course, admit he was an FBI man, and he might not appreciate her help. She would keep her own watch.

Her chief aim was to get a peek at the Kaiglers' living quarters behind the store. It must be from there that intrigue was carried on. The door inside the store was usually closed, and when it was open she couldn't see anything. Every once in a while, however, someone was admitted through a back door that opened from a dusty path behind the store. At those times she wandered down the sidewalk past the rear of the store and looked back. What she hoped to see, what she was certain they had in there, was a wireless, the kind of radio that could transmit back and forth to Germany.

The second thing she observed was the strange procedure of Gordon and Valerie and the others when going to Kaigler's store. The bunch of them would gather at the edge of the woods and stoop, while one of them went across to the store. Darby would keep on with her hopscotch as though she didn't know they were in the world. Sometimes Valerie would catch her eye and wave or say "Hey."

"Oh, hi," Darby would answer, as though she just then saw Valerie. After a time, whoever had crossed as a scout would beckon to the others, and they would all traipse into Kaigler's. Resentment billowed within her. Probably they were spying, too, and since there were so many of them working at it, they would find things out first.

Sometimes Darby saw Yoko heading for the store. She would duck behind Kaigler's to wait until she saw the back of the shiny black head, as Yoko walked home.

Poking around beside the store one day, looking at the bricks for signs of a secret entrance, she saw the man and dog go by, walking down Deckner away from Stewart. She decided to follow him. If she knew where he lived, she would at least know where to run for help if she needed it. He was walking on the sidewalk now, so she switched to the other side and trailed him by a block. Across from Perkerson Park, he turned right, away from the park. She ran then, in case he disappeared before she reached the corner. At the fourth house on the right, he turned in. Casually, she meandered the other way, onto park grounds, and went to the swings for a while, as though that had been her intended destination. You could never tell, she thought, when someone in the spy business was watching. The FBI man could be watching her right now.

Finally she had saved up fifty cents, and she

went to the drugstore to buy her writing paper. The penguin was still blowing smoke rings in the window. There were stacks and stacks of boxes of stationery, and it was as hard to choose as candy from the candy case at Kaigler's. The paper was decorated with all kinds of flowers and designs. Eventually, she chose plain gray, almost like Mother's.

Now that she had her paper, she would have money for candy and could go inside Kaigler's again to spy.

In the days of her loneliness, she wrote her letters to the generals. She used the pen and didn't make a single ink blot. Not knowing where to send them, she had to confide in Mother. Mother suggested that she address them to the Department of the Army in Washington. Addressing letters to Washington made her think of her friends. So now that she had some writing paper of her own, she wrote to Mary and Joyce and Bernie and Joel.

"I have lots of new friends," she wrote. She told about see-sawing with Fancy at school, about eating lemons with Yoko, about Gordon and his polio, and about the Goodbreads' shoot-the-chute. It sounded as though she truly did have lots of friends.

Most days, however, there were no letters to write and spying was a dull business. At least there was Christmas to look forward to. Nothing, not even spies or not having friends, could take the shine off of Christmas.

Every chance she had, she sidled up to Mom and Dad. "I sure hope Santa brings me a panda bear," she'd say. "That's all I want. A panda bear."

"What's a panda bear?" Blair asked.

"It's a particular kind of teddy bear," Darby explained, taking paper and pencil and drawing one as best she could.

"I want one, too," Blair said. Blair was at such an interesting age, Darby thought. One minute she was highly independent, wanting to do everything for herself, and the next minute she was copying everything everyone else said or did.

"Darby, you're too old for a panda bear," Mother said, laughing at Blair.

"But that's all I really want," Darby said.

"I'm not too old," Blair said stoutly, and Mother winked at Darby.

For Mother, the tree was most important. Even if they all went tree hunting together, Mother made the final choice. The tree had to be tall enough to reach the ceiling and perfect all the way around. To Darby, it seemed like giving your best to God.

On Christmas Eve, Darby and Kyla stayed up to decorate the tree after Blair had gone to bed.

This was the most fun of all. Blair knew they had bought the tree, but at their house they pretended it was Santa who decorated it. Daddy wound the lights around, and then they all hung the ornaments. Mother stood back often for an overall view, telling them where to hang something to fill up a space, or where to put a certain color ornament. The icicles were Mother's specialty, because she had the patience to place them one by one in separate strands, hanging straight and not draping across the limbs.

Thinking about the panda bear and knowing he was somewhere in the house kept Darby from going to sleep. In the daytime he would sit royally on her bed, the perfect gift for the Queen of the World. At night, she would hug him goodnight and sit him carefully on her dresser so he wouldn't get messed up. This panda was going to last forever and not get loved to death.

In the morning, before daylight, she woke to the sound of Mother and Blair talking. "You wait," Mother was saying to Blair. "We'll get everyone up and go in at the same time."

"Hurry, hurry, hurry," Blair said.

"I'm up," Darby called, sliding off the bed without using the ladder.

"I'm up," Kyla said, sitting on the side of her

bed. Kyla's Christmas wish was for a small radio of her own.

"I'm not," Dad said, and Darby could picture him rolling over and pulling the pillow over his head. Daddy thought it was absolutely sinful to get up before daylight, even on Christmas.

"Come on, Daddy. Merry Christmas. Merry Christmas." They all gathered around him, tugging off the covers and wrestling the pillow away from him. With Blair and Kyla pulling at his arms and Darby pushing at his back, they moved him to a sitting position. Then he cooperated by sliding his feet into his slippers and shrugging his arms into his robe.

Mother stood at the doorway to the living room, not letting anyone through until everyone was ready. Then she moved aside and let the three girls rush in. Blair didn't know where to look first. Some packages were wrapped and some unwrapped, because Santa's gifts weren't wrapped.

Darby's eyes scanned the room. There he was, her panda. He was the traditional black and white, with a huge red ribbon about his neck, and he was sitting on a little school desk which was, she supposed, for Blair. She gasped and her lungs swelled to the bursting point as she rushed toward her royal bear.

"Darby, those are Blair's things over there," Mother said from the doorway. "Yours are over here." The words didn't penetrate. She was going first to her bear; then she'd see the other things.

"Those are Blair's," Mother said again, but still Darby didn't hear a word of it. Then she scooped up the bear and saw the tag tied to the red ribbon around its neck. "To Blair, from Santa." Darby's eyes, heart, and stomach fell. "He's made a mistake. Santa's made a mistake." Quickly she looked at her mother, wanting the error to be acknowledged and corrected before Blair saw the bear and became attached.

"No, those are Blair's things. Blair? See the big bear? Your things are over here, Darby. You're too old for bears." Mother was smiling, laughing at the magic joy of Christmas morning, teasing, Darby thought.

We'll both have a bear, she thought, following her mother's directions, but she didn't see another bear. If it's not a Santa gift, if it's from Mom and Dad, it will be wrapped. There was no wrapped package big enough for a bear. Fighting with everything in her, she kept back her disappointment and pasted a stiff smile on her face. This was Christmas. This was Jesus's birthday. It was rude to be unhappy with your gifts.

"Oh, it's lovely," she exulted over a new dress.

"So soft," she said about a sweater, holding it to her cheek while she mourned for her bear. "A radio," she said, about the radio from Santa. A radio! This was the mistake. Somehow she had gotten Kyla's radio, and Blair had gotten her bear. She glanced over at Kyla's gifts to look for something that must be Blair's, to make the circle of error complete. But Kyla had a radio, too, and had it plugged in and was hugging it to her ear.

Darby's face was like dried papier mâché. She was grateful she had managed to make a smile before her face hardened, because there was no way she could change her expression now. It was Christmas and she was supposed to be loving and thankful and pray for peace on earth. Behind her stiff Christmas smile she was falling apart.

»17«

"WHAT DID YOU GET for Christmas?" That was the question everyone was asking when school started after the holidays.

"A radio," Darby answered, and the answer drew envious responses.

"Oooooh. Your own radio!"

She had never wanted her own radio. The family radio, which stood on the floor in the living room, had a cloth-covered front on which she could make her own mind pictures of the action. Her new radio was tiny and fit on the top of her dresser. She felt bitter disappointment because she didn't get her panda bear, and guilty because she felt disappointed.

Fancy hadn't been friendly ever since that day Darby had walked home with her, Gordon was hateful, and Yoko was Japanese. After she first mailed the letters to her friends in Washington, she had haunted the mail box, anxious for return mail. Now she dreaded the idea of hearing from them and having to write back again. She could no longer write a happy letter, even by stretching the truth. All the progress she thought she had made in trying to be at home here and make friends had totally evaporated. At recess she watched Fancy play, that white straw hair poking out behind.

LeRoy was talking and talking, like some kind of a parrot, bragging about having a job at the barber shop on the corner.

"I go down there every afternoon to sweep and keep the magazines and newspapers in order. And I can still sell peanuts, too." She didn't know he'd ever sold peanuts and furthermore she didn't care, and she wished he would go away and leave her alone.

Trudging down the dusty pathway after school, she scuffed the toes of her shoes through the dirt and watched puffs like smoke drift around her ankles. This is how Kyla must have felt, walking away from Perkerson School that first day after the entrance tests. If only someone would try to be friends.

As if on cue, someone called from behind her. "Darby. Darby. Hey, wait up." Keeping her face expressionless, not daring to have too much hope, she turned and looked. Above the faces of all the kids walking behind her one by one and two by two, she saw an arm waving. It belonged to Fancy.

"Hey, Darby. Wait on me."

The unusual character of the words hit Darby broadly and stopped her in her tracks. Instead of being happy, she was numb. She didn't even move to the side to let the waves of people by, but stood firmly in the middle of the pathway while they, grumbling, flowed around her as water flows around a boulder in a stream. Wait *on* me? The strange language suddenly choked her—the way they said *hey* instead of *hi*, and *tote* for *carry*. And the hateful *ma'am, ma'am, ma'am*s. And here was Fancy—Fancy, who had stopped being friendly—calling for her to "wait *on* me." Enough was enough. They thought *she* was the strange one, when all the time it was they themselves who were strange.

"I thought for a minute you weren't going to wait," Fancy said, coming up beside her, smiling.

"You thought I wasn't going to wait *on* you?" Darby said, mocking. Every wrong thing that had happened since they had moved to Georgia exploded in her.

Fancy was still smiling. "No, you acted like you were just going to—" she began.

"Do you really want me to wait *on* you?" Darby asked. "You want me to push you down and sit on top of you and wait? Then I'll be waiting *on* you. Is that what you mean? And I won't tote your books, either," Darby snapped, as she stalked down the sidewalk.

"I never asked you to tote my books," Fancy said quietly behind her.

Darby remembered Fancy at the well, and, just like Fancy that day, she did not look back. Down toward Stewart she walked. There, across the street in front of the barber shop, she saw LeRoy with a broom in his hand. He called to her and waved. She pressed her lips together to keep from blowing him the world's loudest raspberry, lifted her hand in a slight wave, and kept on walking.

According to Dad's instructions, she walked on the left-hand side of the road and moved four feet into the brush whenever a car came along. The only day she had ever walked on the other side was the day she had gone to Fancy's. She longed to cross over now, to see what progress had been made on the new house, but she resisted. What if Fancy had wanted to be friends again and she had cut her off with her own hatefulness?

At home she plunked down her books in her room. She wanted to crawl up onto her bunk, but Kyla was already in the room, brooding all over the place. She seemed determined to become a monk.

Darby slipped quietly onto the cold side porch. Winter had finally come to the south, but while everyone else bundled up in coats, a heavy sweater

was enough to keep her plenty warm. People complained of the cold, but they didn't even know
what cold was, Darby thought.

She stood staring over at Yoko's, longing for a
basket swing. A basket swing would be the perfect
place to curl up with her misery. She rejected the
porch furniture and sat cross-legged on the floor,
not minding the cold concrete against her bare
legs. If she were in Washington, everything would
be okay. She would have her friends and her
grandmother, and Dad would take them splashing
across the fords at Rock Creek Park. Maybe they
would even find Blackie Dog.

Here was nowhere, this strange place where
they called her a Yankee and used strange words
and acted hateful to Mr. Kaigler because he used
strange words. Maybe he wasn't really a spy, after
all. Maybe they called him a spy just like they
called her a Yankee. Why were they so afraid of
anyone who wasn't exactly like they were?

Suddenly, Yoko walked out of her house and
down the sidewalk, and crossed to the woods. Uh-
oh, she's coming over, Darby thought, ducking
back into the house and closing the door without a
sound. She slipped into the kitchen and peeped
out the window. Yoko had never come to the
house.

"What are you looking at?" Mother asked.
Darby shook her head and moved away. Yoko was

idly curb walking on the woods side of Stewart Avenue, holding out her hands for balance. She wants me to come out, Darby thought with certainty. Since they went to different schools, it had not been hard to avoid Yoko. Darby moved to the bathroom window and looked again. She remembered the day she'd curb walked with her back to Valerie and Gordon. Was Yoko feeling hollow inside, too? she wondered.

She ducked into her bedroom, picked up her Bible, and walked casually out the back door. Without looking at Yoko, she entered the woods and sat, leaning against her favorite tree. She was reading now in Amos, and she opened the Bible. But instead of looking at it, she looked out from under lowered lids. With the same casual step that Darby herself had used, Yoko came into her range of vision.

"Where've you been?" Darby said, not knowing what else to say.

"Where have *you* been?" Yoko said in return. "I haven't seen you in ages." Yoko paced back and forth a few feet away from Darby. "Have you been mad at me?"

Darby's stomach rolled over at the direct question. "Uh, no. I—I've been busy."

"It's because you think I'm Japanese, isn't it?" Yoko said. Darby tried to think of a denial, but none would come. "I know it is. Everyone feels that way. Since the war started, I don't even have any friends anymore. Just because of the way I look. I couldn't speak Japanese if I had to. Daddy says you look Irish. How would you like it if we were at war with Ireland and everybody hated you because you have blue eyes and blonde hair and freckles?"

Darby was astonished at the barrage of words. She was not Irish, although some of her ancestors had come over from Ireland. But that was years ago. And yet, she might as well be a foreigner; everyone hated her, anyway. Except for Yoko, who was as friendless as she.

"Do you know they even throw rocks at me?"

Darby looked up. "No!" she said in horror, thinking of herself smashing Japanese cups and saucers against the sidewalk. "Is everybody crazy?" she said. Suddenly she understood why Yoko didn't go to the movies. People, including herself, insisted on making Yoko into the enemy and Yoko didn't have anything to do with the enemy. Darby wanted to jump up and hug Yoko. Instead, she pointed to her Bible. "I have to do my Bible readings. I'm on Amos. Do you want to read Amos with me?"

Yoko nodded. "Do you want to come to the swing?"

Darby nodded and stood up. They crossed

Stewart and curled up together in the basket swing, alternating verses as they read.

"Listen to this," Yoko said. " 'I was an herdsman and a gatherer of sycamore fruit!' "

"Where? Let me see." Yoko put her finger under the verse and they looked at each other in amazement. "Amos was a gatherer of sycamore fruit," they said together. Those words were somehow a sign, a sign that they were supposed to be friends.

Without saying a word to each other, Darby and Yoko jumped from the swing and raced around back to the tree. With Muffin behind them, they scrambled up to comfortable positions. Darby looked at Yoko, breathless and happy.

"Just a minute," Yoko said. "I have to get some lemons." Yoko climbed down from the tree, ran into the house, and reappeared with two lemons, the salt shaker, and a knife. Yoko cut one lemon and salted both halves. She handed one half to Darby.

Darby and Yoko sank their teeth into their salted lemons at the same time. In a minute they returned to the verse they had left off with. " 'I was an herdsman and a gatherer of sycamore fruit.' "

» 18 «

HAVING RENEWED HER FRIENDSHIP with Yoko, Darby wanted to do the same with Fancy, too. Instead of just watching the bouncing white-blonde hair on the playground, Darby abandoned the see-saw line and went after Fancy.

"I'm sorry about yesterday," she said.

"You are? You truly are?" Fancy looked at Darby with soft blue eyes, searching for truth.

"I was very rude," Darby said.

"Yes, you were."

"I apologize. I thought maybe we could be friends again."

"If you want to," Fancy said hesitantly.

"That's what I'm saying it for."

They grasped hands and twirled around, heads under arms, in the fastest "washing machine" turns that Darby had ever done. They collapsed into giggles. Darby was so happy, she could scarcely recall how miserable she had been just yesterday.

"Come home with me this afternoon," Fancy said. Darby hunched her shoulders, remembering the awkward feelings when she had gone before.

"Come see the house," Fancy said. "Daddy hasn't finished yet, but we've moved in, anyway."

"But your father doesn't like city people," she said. She had never understood that remark of Fancy's, but she knew it had something to do with what had gone wrong between them.

"Oh, you're county people," Fancy said. "Besides, we feel like city people in our new house."

On Stewart Avenue they both spotted a red Lucky Strike package at the same time. Racing to it, they tried to bump each other out of the way. Fancy got her foot on it first.

"It has two lucks," Darby said, stomping and twirling when Fancy was through.

"Three," Fancy said, twirling again.

"Four!" Darby twirled again, and they started laughing.

"I say five and that's all," Fancy said, taking a final twirl.

"Can you come to Sunday school with me Sunday?" Darby asked. Fancy looked at her with surprise and pleasure.

"Ooh, I'd like to. You ask. Come on." Fancy raced across Stewart Avenue and started down the bank toward the playhouse.

The little house looked abandoned, as though no one had played there for years. Darby started to say, "Don't you play in the playhouse anymore?" But when she parted her lips to say it, she suddenly understood everything. Her own exact words echoed in her head—"Oh, a playhouse." Her breath came hard, and she looked at Fancy, who was moving happily down the hill. The teeny house was not a playhouse. It had been Fancy's real house.

Beyond the old house was a beautiful new house, with unpainted yellow boards gleaming and a roof reaching for the sky. "Is that it?" Darby asked in wonder.

"I don't see another," Fancy said. Mesmerized, Darby walked toward the house and touched the corner boards. Fancy's mother came to the door, wiping her hands on an apron. Sounds of hammering echoed from the house.

"He ain't finished yet. Things is still a mess," Mrs. Potter said, as she opened the door for the girls to come in.

"What's not finished?" Darby asked. Everything was beautiful. She stepped into the kitchen to look at the kitchen sink and the cabinets. From there she could see all the skeletal boards of the inside of the house.

"The walls aren't finished," Fancy said.

"The walls?" Darby thought Fancy had almost said dumbo at the end of her statement, but she was too entranced at the idea of a man building his own house to even mind. She loved the way the studs striped the inside walls, and if it were her house she would not want them covered. "Would he mind—would he get mad if I watched?"

"You want to watch?" Fancy asked in surprise. "I'm sick and tired of watching, myself. Sick and tired of helping."

"You help?" Darby's excitement grew at the thought of being able to help build a house.

"I hand him stuff. Nails. Tools. Come on." Darby followed Fancy through the narrow hallway into a skeleton of a room, where Mr. Potter was working on the stud framing. The girls stood in the doorway. Mr. Potter kept working without acknowledging them. Fancy turned back toward the kitchen, and Darby reluctantly followed.

"Mom, Darby wants to ask you something."

Darby shrank. "Me?" she whispered to Fancy. "You ask."

"No, you," Fancy whispered back. "She's more likely to let me if you ask."

"Uh," Darby said, looking from Fancy to Mrs.

Potter. "Uh, ma'am"—she managed to make the hated word come off her tongue—"I was wondering if . . . uh . . . I mean I want to know, can Fancy come to Sunday school with me next Sunday? It's all right with my mother and father." She figured it would help to add that, and she asked forgiveness for the lie, even though she was sure it would be all right with Mom and Dad. This wasn't anything like trick or treating or going to the trestle after dark.

Mrs. Potter looked from one girl to the other. Fancy was wringing her hands and looking at her mother with the most imploring look. "Fancy has her own Sunday school to go to," Mrs. Potter said.

"But if I go with her one Sunday maybe she can come with me one Sunday," Fancy burst forth.

"Yes," Darby said eagerly, smiling at Fancy for the brilliant idea. "If she comes with me one Sunday, maybe I can go with her one Sunday."

Mrs. Potter looked doubtful.

"I want to go, too," said one of the little boys.

"You're not invited," Fancy said, rubbing his head. "Will you ask Daddy?" Mrs. Potter nodded and walked down the hallway. Fancy thrust crossed fingers in front of Darby's face. Even though they strained to hear, all Darby heard was murmuring.

Mrs. Potter came back looking very solemn but

nodding her head. "Okay," she said. "He said okay and maybe you could spend the night when you come. We'd like that."

"Wow, thanks, Mrs. Potter," Darby said. "Ma'am," she added. "Do you need any water? I'll be glad to bring you a bucket of water."

"I don't need it now," Mrs. Potter said, going to the sink and turning the faucet.

"Oh! The water's hooked up," Fancy said with delight, reaching for the faucet and turning the flow of water on and off, on and off.

Darby kept the smile on her face and didn't show her disappointment, since Mrs. Potter and Fancy were obviously so pleased. It would be much more fun, Darby thought, to get your water from a well. "Can I draw a bucket, anyway?" Darby asked, looking from Mrs. Potter to Fancy.

Fancy stretched her arms, palms up. "Sure, why not."

"Thanks a lot," Darby shouted, and burst from the house. At the well, she lifted the bucket from its holding nail and carefully wound the handle, lowering the bucket. What she still didn't understand was how the water got into the bucket. She didn't want to embarrass herself by drawing an empty bucket. She turned to ask Fancy, but Fancy was dawdling, doing something on the other side of the yard. The bucket splashed into the water.

Darby waited a minute and then began rewinding. The winding was harder coming up than going down. The bucket must be full.

"It's got water in it," Darby said proudly, when Fancy came up beside her and leaned over, looking into the well.

"What did you think it had? Elephants?"

"It weighs like an elephant," Darby said.

" 'Course. Water's heavy. I ought to know, I've carried enough bucketsful."

"How does the water get in the bucket?"

"What?" Fancy stared at Darby. "Just what is it you don't understand? You let the bucket down, it fills with water, and you bring it back up."

"Yes, but if the bucket goes down right side up, how does the water get in?" The bucket was in sight now and Darby was relieved. The water was heavy and the winding took a lot of strength. She was afraid she would let it slip.

Fancy was laughing, shaking her head in wonder at Darby's ignorance. As the bucket neared the top, Fancy reached out, grabbed the sides of the bucket with both hands and brought it over to rest on the ledge.

"Here," Fancy said, handing Darby a dipper. "What happens, you see, is that when the bucket hits the water, it tips over." Fancy was demonstrating with her hands. "And when it tips over, it begins to fill with water until it sinks and fills full. Then, when you rewind the rope it rises right up to the top like magic. You see?" Fancy was grinning. "Drink up," she said, moving Darby's hand to dip the dipper into the bucket.

Darby drank a dipper full. The water was as cold as from the refrigerator and was the best water she had ever tasted. Fancy redipped the dipper, drank a few sips, and tossed the rest into the yard with a splat.

·» 19 «·

When Fancy came walking up Athens Avenue on Sunday, Darby, who was waiting on her front steps, almost didn't recognize her. "Is that you?" she asked, as the girl with whitish-blonde curly hair and a yellow pinafore stepped into the yard. Fancy looked fluffy enough to float away.

"I always dress up on Sundays," Fancy said, sounding as soft as she looked, "to look my best for Jesus."

"You look beautiful," Darby said, amazed at the difference between this Sunday Fancy and the girl who chased wildly around the school yard. Mother often tried to persuade Darby to curl her hair, but Darby didn't want any messing with her hair, except to pigtail it when it was long enough.

Walking up the street, Darby imagined faces at

SALTED LEMONS **141**

every window. The people of Athens Avenue had probably never seen anything as magnificent as Fancy, who matched the bright and springlike winter day. Darby herself wore a short-sleeved dress, amazed at going bare-armed in January. Some days were cold, but Dad said it never would snow enough for sledding.

One block up, they saw the man with the huge white dog turn the corner onto Athens.

"Oh, Darby, look," Fancy said, and took a fast step toward the dog.

"Don't, Fancy," Darby said, putting a hand on Fancy's arm.

"Why not?" Fancy said indignantly.

"He's an FBI man," Darby whispered.

"So what? If he's FBI, he's on our side," Fancy said and walked hurriedly toward the approaching man.

"Your dog is so beautiful," Fancy said to the man. "May I pet him?" Darby lagged behind, admiring the magnificent animal but afraid of the man.

"Certainly," the man said to Fancy. "Her name is Greta and she's very gentle." Fancy began patting Greta and rubbing her fingers through the fur. Darby came up behind Fancy, keeping Fancy between herself and the man. The only dog she'd touched since Blackie Dog was Yoko's Muffin, and she was very envious of Fancy.

"Come on, Darby, I thought you loved dogs," Fancy said.

"Don't be afraid just because she's big," the man said.

"What kind of dog is she?" Darby managed to ask, still remaining behind Fancy. If they interpreted her behavior as fear of the dog, so much the better. As much as she wanted to pet the dog, touching it would be like touching the man himself.

"A Samoyed," he said. "Samoyed. She's going to have puppies any day."

"Is she a sled dog?" Fancy asked.

"She's not," the man said, "but many Samoyeds are. And they're used as herding dogs, too." During the conversation they had sort of swapped places on the sidewalk, so that now Darby and Fancy were uphill of the man and dog.

"She sure is pretty," Fancy said once more, removing her hand from Greta's fur and moving on. "What's the matter with you?" Fancy asked, as they went on their way. Darby could not explain what was the matter, why she was afraid of an FBI man. He was, as Fancy had said, on their side. She turned once, to look back at the dog. How she missed Blackie Dog. How she wished for a dog, even though she knew she couldn't have one. A panda would do, but how would she get one? Her birthday wasn't until summer.

At Sunday school, the Boys' Bataan Prayer Band swarmed around, waiting to be introduced to Fancy. "Get her to come every Sunday and you can be in our Prayer Band," one boy whispered. Little holy snob, Darby thought.

"I've read the last of Amos, Jonah, and all the way to the end of the Old Testament, and the first seven chapters of Matthew," she said, when it was her turn for the week's accounting. Each week, the sound of awe that greeted the recital of her list of Bible readings filled her with pleasure.

This week's readings had been momentous because she had completed the Old Testament on Friday. She loved the Old Testament, especially the story of Jonah. Darby thought Jonah was immensely brave to admit he had been the cause of the storm, and to tell the people on the ship to cast him into the sea. But getting into the New Testament and reading the actual words of Jesus in red letters had nearly made her breathless.

"What about Obadiah?" asked the teacher, who was checking.

"I read Obadiah before," Darby said. "I read it

out of order." Blessed Obadiah, the book with only one chapter.

"Now, Darby," the teacher said gently, "I know it is quite an undertaking for a ten-year-old to read the Bible all the way through. In fact, it's really too much. But you mustn't, ah, pretend to read parts you haven't read."

"But I *have* read Obadiah," she said. "I read Obadiah near the first."

"Well, tell me something about it."

Darby opened and closed her mouth like a goldfish. She was prepared to tell about Amos and Jonah and even about Micah wailing like the dragons and mourning like the owls. Obadiah, however, she had read a long time ago, and all she could remember about it was that it had only one chapter.

"What good is it for you to read it if you don't know what you've read?"

The voice was gentle but the accusation stabbed Darby. What good indeed? Did they think she could memorize the whole Bible? Wasn't it enough to be faithful and struggle through it? And why an inquisition on this day, of all days, when Fancy was here?

"Obadiah has only one chapter," she said, since it was all she could remember.

"Now, see?" the teacher said. "None of the Old Testament books are that short."

Darby closed her eyes and slowly reopened them. "Obadiah has only one chapter," she repeated. "If I were going to cheat, I would have cheated on Psalms."

The teacher thumbed through the Bible. The book of Obadiah was so short that she missed it going and coming. "Well, so it does," the woman said, after checking and rechecking, perhaps to be sure that pages weren't missing from her Bible. "Now, tell me one thing from Obadiah."

Darby's ears burned. Fire touched her from Fancy's bright yellow dress. All the world was holding its breath and waiting for her answer. Darby strained her memory. Wasn't Obadiah the one with the heathen? She remembered discussing it with Yoko. "The heathen," she blurted.

"Yes, it does talk about the heathen," the woman said, walking over and giving Darby a quick hug. "I'm sure you did read it, and I apologize for doubting you. We're all very proud of you."

"Your visitor. Your visitor," someone said from behind her. The teacher then checked Fancy out as a visitor and added more points. Darby wanted to say she hadn't brought a visitor for points. In fact, she wanted to take back all her points. Hugs and sorry's didn't make up for being shamed in front of everyone. She kept her memory verses to herself, including the beautiful one about the owls and dragons.

In her yellow dress, matching the yellow Sunday school classroom, Fancy was the one who looked like Queen of the World. Some of the girls were huffy over the attention Fancy was receiving from the boys.

"Fancy. What kind of name is that?" one girl asked rudely.

"You don't have to answer," Darby said, regaining her own confidence and feeling proud because Fancy was her visitor. But Fancy was already answering, as politely and regally as a true queen.

"It's short for Frances," Fancy said. "My little brother couldn't say Frances." Darby, who'd never known that Fancy's name wasn't Fancy, smiled at the ordinariness of it.

» 20 «

WHEN SHE WALKED into Kaigler's, Darby always pressed her hand firmly against the "Colonial is good bread" bar. Touching it, reminding herself of her stupidity and humiliation, was a way of forgiving herself. As she entered the dim store today, she stopped short of the counter.

The FBI man was standing at the counter with Greta. He was talking to Mr. Kaigler, and Mr. Kaigler was smiling and looking more pleasant than she had ever seen him. She forgot she had decided that Mr. Kaigler probably wasn't a spy, after all. Seeing the two men together, she suddenly thought that the man with the dog was not an FBI man at all, but a fellow spy of Mr. Kaigler's. She was torn between wanting to leave quickly and wanting to be close enough to hear their conversation. She took an orange drink from

147

the cold-drink chest, opened it, and eased toward the counter, without getting too close.

"What's the matter, *Blümchen?*" Mr. Kaigler said. "You afraid of the dog? Come on over. Greta's a wonderful dog. She won't hurt you."

Stiffly, she moved toward them so they wouldn't suspect that she suspected.

"Come on, *Blümchen.*" Mr. Kaigler came out from behind the counter, took her arm, and led her toward the dog. "See? Greta won't hurt you, will you, Greta?" He took her hand and pressed it into the animal's fur. "I don't usually allow dogs in here, but Greta is special. Right, *Blümchen?*"

Darby tried to withdraw. At least they thought it was the dog she was afraid of.

"She's a Samoyed," Mr. Kaigler said. "Isn't she exquisite?"

Greta's owner gave her some commands. "Sit." "Down." "Speak." Greta obeyed instantly, and Darby thought it was a shame for such a fine dog to be wasted on spies. "She's just had pups," Mr. Kaigler said, "and I'm getting one."

"Oh?" Darby said. Thinking about dogs and puppies released her from fear. "I wish I had a puppy," she said, now looking at Greta wistfully.

"Well, dogs like Greta cost a lot of money," Mr. Kaigler said. "More than the pennies you have when you come in here to buy a fistful of candies.

Greta's pup will be the first dog I've ever had. I've waited all my life."

Well, at least she'd had Blackie Dog, Darby thought. She felt a tenderness toward Mr. Kaigler until she suddenly remembered she was with spies. She forgot about her Mary Janes and held out a nickel to Mr. Kaigler, wanting him to take it quickly so she could run.

"Oh, no, *Blümchen*," he said with a big smile. "That orange is on me, and you'd better drink up before it gets hot. Nothing worse than a hot cold drink."

She stood there with the nickel in her palm, not wanting to take anything from a spy, but he closed her fingers around the nickel and she turned and dashed out without even saying thanks. She heard them laughing behind her.

At the edge of the woods across from the store, all the kids from Athens Avenue were huddled down, as if they were hiding. Darby almost laughed. There was no place to hide in those thin woods, even in the summer when the trees were leafed out.

"What's going on?" Darby asked, crossing the street and going directly toward them.

"Are there any city kids in the store?" Valerie asked.

"No, why?"

"Oh, good. You're sure?" The group rose from their huddle and moved toward the street.

"You mean—" Darby started and stopped. Was that the reason for their strange manner of going to the store?

"They throw rocks at us," John Goodbread said.

"Yeah, and don't forget you throw rocks at them," Valerie said.

"What is all this rock throwing business?" Darby asked. "They throw rocks at you. You throw rocks at them. Everyone throws rocks at Yoko Sasaki."

"I don't!" Valerie said quickly.

"I don't." "I don't," the others said, one on top of the other.

"But she's Japanese!" John Goodbread said, as though he had something distasteful in his mouth.

"She's not!" Darby said.

"Listen to the dumb Yankee talk," Gordon said. They hadn't called her Yankee for a long time and the word stung.

"Not Japanese? Where'd she get that black hair?"

"And those slant eyes?"

"And that yellow skin?"

"The government's going to make her move."

"They're rounding up all the Japanese."

"But Yoko is not Japanese," Darby insisted. "Her heritage is Japanese. But she's as American as you and me. She has lived right there since she was born." She pointed toward the white stucco house.

"Well, let's go to the store," Sonny said, changing the subject.

"Valerie, you run over and see if it's still safe," Gordon said.

"And all this time I thought you were spying!" Darby said.

"Well, we are," Jim said. "We're spying on the spies."

"Spies? Plural spy? How many are there?" Darby was teasing now. They were afraid of the city kids. Well, she certainly wasn't afraid of city kids, but that did explain why the kids at Sunday school were not friendly. She had never applied it to them. They were city. She was county.

"There's at least one spy besides Mr. Kaigler," said John Goodbread, sounding self-important. "He hangs around the store a lot, waiting to exchange messages with Mr. Kaigler."

"I know," Darby said. So apparently they also thought the FBI man was a spy. "He's in there right now."

"With his white chow," Valerie said, returning with an all-clear report. All clear of city children but not of spies.

"Yep, that's him," Darby said. In this bright sunshine the idea of spies seemed ridiculous. Spies and city and county and Japanese, and all of them throwing rocks at each other.

"Except it's a German shepherd, not a chow," Gordon corrected.

Darby almost laughed. "It's neither one," she said. "It's a Samoyed." They all heaved shoulders and sighed at her.

"Whoever heard of that?" they said.

"You know Darby," Gordon added. "She always has to act like she knows the most."

Darby shrugged.

"You were in there with them. Did you hear what they were saying?" Jim and John and Valerie asked all at once.

"What were they talking about?" Gordon asked, and she stared at him because he, General Gordon himself in person, had spoken to her directly. She looked over at the store. The bricks were bathed in winter sunshine, and the afternoon light cast shadows to the east. The shape of the store fell across Stewart Avenue. "Dogs," she said, realizing they'd said absolutely nothing to make her suspect them. "They were talking about dogs."

"Is that all?"

"Well, what do you expect?" Sonny said. "If he's really a spy, he wouldn't be saying anything suspicious where someone could hear."

"Right," Gordon shouted. "That proves it."

"That does *not* prove he's a spy. I go in there and don't act suspicious," Darby said. "Does that make me a spy?"

"Nobody would think you were a spy," Gordon said.

"Who says?" she said.

"Whose mouth was moving when you heard it?" he said. "Who ever heard of a girl spy?"

"Didn't you ever hear of Mata Hari?" Darby asked.

"No," they said. "Is that something else you made up?" It would be useless, she decided, to tell them about the woman spy from World War I. They would not believe her.

"I can spy as good as you any day," she said instead.

"Cannot."

"Can too."

"Cannot."

"Can too."

"You were too scared to even go to the trestle."

"You know it was because my father wouldn't let me," she said. "I'll go to the trestle any time you say."

"Okay. How about Friday night?" Gordon said. "At midnight."

A collective gasp arose from the group. How could she possibly go at midnight when Dad wouldn't even let her go at nine o'clock? But some-

how she'd do it. She'd sneak out. She had to show
Gordon she was Queen of the World.

"Okay," she said, and they all gasped again.

Just then the man came out of the store with
Greta and started down the street. Darby gave him
a small, shy wave, which he returned as he walked
in long strides to keep up with his dog. On the opposite side of the street, Gordon and the others
followed a block behind, spying. She stood, watching them go.

» 21 «

ON FRIDAY NIGHTS, Darby could stay up until ten o'clock. Usually the evening passed quickly. But tonight, even though she listened to "Sherlock Holmes," "Gangbusters," and "People Are Funny" on the radio, the time seemed to pass slowly. When she went to bed, she stared at the ceiling three feet above her head. If she fell asleep she would not wake up, and if she set the alarm her parents—and Kyla, too, of course—would hear it.

Through the window she saw the black silhouette of the bare trees against the sky. Sometimes without thinking she'd done things against her parents' wishes, but this was the first time she had planned to do something she knew they wouldn't like. She would like to have told them, but it was impossible. She reviewed the day she had walked under the trestle and vowed not to be afraid.

At twenty until twelve she slipped from her bed, easing slowly so the springs wouldn't creak. She picked up her dress from the chair, where she had supposedly left it carelessly. She slipped her sockless feet into her shoes. When she peeped out the door she was relieved to see only the bathroom light on. It was left on all night, in case Blair needed to go to the bathroom. Her parents' bed-room door was closed and no line of light showed from underneath.

In the bathroom, she put on her dress and tied her shoes. Her ankles looked pale and skinny and bare without socks. Properly dressed children always wore socks, Mother insisted. Properly man-nered children always said *ma'am,* Miss Hardy said. Proper children did not sneak out of the house at midnight, either, she thought. Well, per-haps no one would be at the corner, and she could come back home and go to bed and tomorrow call Gordon coward, chicken, and yellow.

She and the Goodbreads nearly scared each other, creeping across behind their houses. Gor-don and Valerie and Sonny were already on the corner.

"Ready?" Gordon whispered.

What do you think I'm here for if I'm not ready? she thought. But she responded as he wished by saying, "Ready."

"What if someone sees us?" Jim Goodbread asked.

"Don't think about it," Gordon said. "Just walk along as though it's afternoon." They crossed Deckner and started up the gradual hill of Athens. This was the way she walked to Sunday school, and she was familiar with every step of the way. But it was scary at midnight.

"So, we're really going to do it," Valerie said, as they approached the corner of the drugstore. "We didn't do it on Halloween," she said to Darby. Darby blinked.

"You shut up," Gordon said.

"Well, we didn't," Valerie said. So that little stink, Darby thought. He had called her all kinds of names and he hadn't even done it himself.

"I think I'm going home," Jim said.

"Oh, no, you're not," John said, grabbing the back of Jim's shirt.

"This time we're going to do it," Gordon said. "You're not going to be chicken, are you?"

Darby glared at him. She had not said one thing to indicate she was scared, even though she was. The only thing that would stop her was if she dropped dead of fright, she thought. Otherwise, she was going on. As they passed the drugstore and came in sight of the trestle, their steps shortened to inches per step. In the illumination of the streetlight, Darby looked for and found the same old Lucky Strike package that had been there over two months ago. She stepped on it, twirled, and proclaimed her luck.

The others ignored her. "Have you ever heard her scream?" Jim asked everyone.

"No, but they say her scream will make your blood turn to ice," John said. "Sometimes you just go into shock and can't even run and they find your body later."

"Aw, I don't believe any of that," Gordon said, thrusting back his shoulders and picking up a regular walking speed. Darby thrust her shoulders back, also, and kept pace with him. The two of them were under the trestle for a minute or two before the others joined them.

"It sure took you long enough," Darby said.

"Shhh," Sonny said.

"Shhh, what?" Darby said.

"You're supposed to be quiet."

"Who says?"

"I say," Gordon put in. "I'm the commanding officer and I say be quiet. We have to listen for her scream."

"You mean she screams quietly?" Darby asked, delighted because Gordon was forgetting to filter his words through Valerie.

"Will you shut up?" Jim said. "She could be

sneaking up on us right now and we wouldn't even hear her."

"You can't hear a ghost sneak," Darby hissed.

"Shhh!" Gordon put his finger to his lips and moved his eyes furtively.

"Yes, General," she said. As soon as the sound of her own voice left her ears, a clunking sound entered. It had come from up on the trestle. A nearby street light suddenly went out, and darkness and silence enveloped them. Darby shivered.

"It was just the track creaking," John said.

"Tracks don't creak," Jim said.

"They do if a train is coming."

"Oh." They all sighed in relief.

"I don't hear it," Jim said.

"Be quiet and you will." All of them became silent, but they heard no rickety-rackety vibration from an approaching train. What they heard was a crunch on the gravel of the embankment, then a sliding sound.

"That's no train," Jim breathed, and he darted out from under the trestle. Sonny grabbed for him but missed.

"Oh, let him go. He's just a flunky, anyway."

"What was it, though?"

"Shut *up!*" They huddled silently as Jim made his way to the drugstore corner, where he stood under the next street light.

"Has it been fifteen minutes?" John asked.

"Five," Gordon answered, after a glance at his watch.

"And you're supposed to be quiet!" Sonny said.

Darby examined the faces of the group huddled under the railroad trestle in the dark. Suddenly, a high, piercing scream came from their midst. In an instant, all but Darby had bolted out from under the trestle. Darby was left standing by herself.

"Darby, Darby, come on!" they shouted at her from the distance.

"I can't," she whispered hoarsely. "My blood's turned to ice." Uncertainly, they darted toward her, then turned away, first one, then the other, wanting to help but afraid, perhaps, that if they touched her, their blood, too, would turn to ice. Finally, Jim Goodbread, who'd come running from the drugstore corner, grabbed her hand and dragged her out from under the trestle. At the corner she could hold it no longer and she split the air with laughter. They were as startled by the laughter as they had been by the scream.

"Is her hair turning white?" Jim asked.

They think I've gone mad, she thought. "It was me," she said, as they stood under the street light. "It was me who screamed," she repeated.

They stared at her, not understanding. "We'd

better get her home," Gordon said. They gathered around her and began shepherding her.

"No," she said. "We've got to go back."

"She's gone off for sure," John said, and they closed in tightly. She jerked loose and ran back toward the trestle.

"It's not fifteen minutes yet," she called to them. "If I don't stay fifteen minutes, you'll say it doesn't count." Somehow it was less frightening to be standing there by herself. They had done a good job of scaring each other under the trestle.

"You mean it really was you?" Valerie said. To prove it, Darby peeled off another scream. Even though they saw her do it, they flinched.

"Shut up, Darby," they said, covering their ears with their hands.

"Come on, Darby, let's go."

"Is it fifteen minutes?"

"It's time enough," Gordon said. "And if I say it's time enough, then it's time enough."

"Am I the bravest?" she said, as she walked toward them.

"No, I'm the bravest," Jim said. "I'm the only one who would rescue you." The others laughed, nervously, embarrassed because they hadn't helped her.

"We'll be the bravest together," Darby said to Jim, putting her arm through his.

"Oh, no," he said, twisting free of her grip, "because as soon as I get my strength back I'm going to kill you!"

His threat did not dim her delight, and she looked for the Lucky Strike package, stomped her foot on it, and twirled three times. "My luck. My luck. My luck," she said as she turned. "My own personal very best luck."

» 22 «

AN AMAZING THING happened on Saturday. About an hour before their usual time to go to the movies, Gordon, the general himself, came over and asked Darby to go with them. She stood in the doorway looking at him, smiling in surprise and wishing she could think of some queenly, withering thing to say. But the truth was, she did want to go to the movies and wanted very much to go with them. Mother gave her fifteen cents. The movie cost nine cents and that left six cents for candy. She went to Kaigler's for a sackful of licorice stars, because they would last the longest.

"I'm going to the movies," she said to Mr. Kaigler, astonishing herself by talking to him in a friendly tone.

"Ah, *Blümchen,* at last you have friends to go with to the movies," he said. She looked at him, puzzled, smiling. How did he know? "Ah," he said,

"I know why you come to Kaigler's at two o'clock every Saturday. I know the lonely Saturdays."

In spite of his gruff voice, she felt a rough comfort with him. She was ashamed of herself for having been frightened of him just because he sounded different. Surely he was not a spy.

When she met Gordon and the others on the corner, Gordon said, "And how is the spy today?"

"He's not a spy," she said.

"Is too."

"Is not."

"Is too."

"Is not."

In spite of this exchange the new friendship between them was not destroyed. He even walked beside her on the sidewalk.

"Was it awful to have polio?" she asked him, as they tromped down Deckner.

"Awful," he said. "I thought I was going to die." She matched her step to his, left, right, left, right, to get the feel of his limp. What was it like, she wondered, to think you were going to die? Valerie and Sonny and Jim and John filled the air with talk about the upcoming movie, so it was difficult to think about death.

In the theater, Darby somehow wound up in the lead. She walked to the center of the theater and moved left into the middle section.

"No, not here," Valerie said. "The city kids sit here." Darby turned to look at Valerie and saw that the boys had already walked past her and were sitting closer to the front, over in the right-hand section. She looked around the theater at the separate groups of children. Was there an imaginary line even in the movie theater?

Darby followed Valerie to where the boys sat, and she curled up in her seat. Sonny sat on Darby's right, scrunched down in the seat with his knees propped against the back of the seat in front of him. Darby thought it looked like the most marvelously casual position, but when she tried it she almost disappeared down into her chair. She drew her legs up under her and became engrossed in the wonders of the screen.

Valerie was a little disappointed because it was not a Hopalong Cassidy movie. But Darby had not been to many movies, and as Roy Rogers tromped across the screen with Trigger, she thought that there couldn't be anything better. To have a horse like Trigger, a fat funny friend like Smiley Burnette, and be able to sing was everything. In the Sylvan Theater, eating licorice stars, Darby fell in love with Roy Rogers.

The weekly serial was about Shana, girl of the jungle. Each episode ended with the hero or heroine in a dangerous position. And the next one started at that very point. This time the story ended with Shana tied to a runaway mine car. On the way home they discussed plans for reenacting the drama.

"Let's let Darby be Shana," Valerie said. Darby looked from one to the other, glowing in the warmth of their nodding acceptance.

Through the thin woods between Athens and Stewart, the bad guys chased her. Finally the villains caught her, and she struggled and fought as they dragged her toward the Goodbreads' shoot-the-chute.

"You'll never get away with this," Shana said boldly.

"No one will ever find you here," said one of the villains. At the bottom of the ladder, she was still putting up a fight.

"Go on, Darby, climb up," Gordon said.

"Shana wouldn't climb up," she said. "They'd have to take her." It disgruntled her to have to step out of character for a petty explanation.

"You know we can't carry you up the ladder," Sonny said. "If you won't climb, we'll let Valerie be Shana."

"You said I could be, and I'm going to be," Darby said, mounting the ladder to the six-foot platform.

From there, they wrestled her onto the flat cart.

Then they discussed the ways of securing her to the cart.

"Chain her," said John, dangling a chain.

"No. We can't chain her or tie her," Jim protested. "It might be dangerous. If the cart slipped off the track she couldn't jump clear."

"The cart has never come off the track," John said.

"Tie me," Darby said, disgusted. Did they think Shana would not get away if she wasn't tied?

They tied her hands behind her and bound her ankles together. Then they began tying her feet to the cart. Suddenly she felt too tightly bound.

"Maybe I should have my hands free," she suggested.

"Holy cow," Valerie said. "You were the one who wanted to be tied up."

"But what if there's an accident?" Jim said, from where he was balancing on the cross bracing at the side of the platform.

"There's never been an accident," John said scornfully, as he and Sonny untied her hands. "No one's ever been hurt, even."

"My feet, too," Darby said, feeling a little foolish but wanting to be ready for a swift spring away, just in case.

"You'll escape," said Gordon suspiciously.

"No, I won't, I promise. I'll do it just like the

show." Finally they decided to tie one ankle to the cart. Then they became Shana and the villains again.

"This will be the end of Shana, girl of the jungle," the villains cried.

"You won't get away with this," Shana insisted to the last.

"She won't bother us anymore. Now we can get the diamonds."

In the very next second, Darby saw diamonds. The cart shot straight out, jerking her sideways. Sparkles of color exploded from her eyes, and she was falling and falling and falling. Screams surrounded her like the stars, piercing her.

Slowly it came to her that she was no longer falling. Now she was swaying back and forth above the ground, which was just beyond her fingertips. Knees and legs surrounded her now.

"Get her down."

"I can't."

"Get your mother."

"Mother!"

"Mother!"

"Mrs. Goodbread!"

"What's holding me here?" Darby cried, wondering how much longer she had to live.

"The chain," Valerie said, shifting from one foot to the other and reaching out to Darby but not daring to touch her. Darby bent her neck and looked up. She saw that she was dangling by the ankle. The cart was banging against her legs and bottom. She was secured to the cart by the rope and the cart was secured to the platform by the chain.

"Who chained me?" she screamed, suddenly realizing you didn't have to have polio to be crippled. Squeezing her eyes shut, she saw the shattered bones and the months and months and months she wouldn't be able to walk.

Mrs. Goodbread came flying out the back door. "Where are you hurt?" she asked, holding Darby gently to stop the swaying, which none of the others had thought to do.

"My leg. My leg," Darby cried.

"How about your shoulders? Your back? I need to know where I can hold you while they untie you. And who did this?"

"I don't know. I don't know," Darby cried softly. Her back? Oh, her back. If something happened to her back, that could be forever. She began to sob as Mrs. Goodbread poked and prodded, trying to determine her injuries.

There was no special pain in her shoulders or back, so Mrs. Goodbread boosted her to make enough slack for someone to unhook the chain. Many arms reached to help set her right side up on the ground, in a sitting position.

"Who did that to her? What is wrong with you,

to do such a thing!" Mrs. Goodbread demanded.

"I didn't," Valerie said.

"I didn't," Sonny said. They both stepped back, as though space would confirm their innocence.

Gordon, Jim, and John added their "I didn't"s.

"I was just supposed to be tied to the cart," Darby said. They had lowered the cart with her and she was still tied to it. She stretched out her leg, as Gordon untied the rope. "Is it broken?" she asked Mrs. Goodbread, who was lightly pressing fingers around Darby's ankle.

"I don't think so. See if you can stand." They helped her to her feet. To her amazement she could stand, and it didn't even hurt much.

They hovered around her while she shook herself out, checking muscles and bones at Mrs. Goodbread's direction. Which one of them had chained the cart to the platform? Gordon? Was he just pretending to be a friend so he could do something worse than merely ignore her?

» 23 «

ALL WEEKEND, Valerie, Gordon, Jim, John, Sonny, and Mr. and Mrs. Goodbread kept coming over to see if Darby was really all right. Instead of enjoying the attention, Darby became uneasy and suspicious. The Goodbreads probably thought it was one of their boys who'd chained the cart to the platform. Had one of them confessed? Jim had threatened her because she'd frightened them at the trestle, but Jim was the gentle one. Perhaps it was John. The only one she was sure it was not, was Valerie. And she didn't think it was Sonny. But they were all acting as though nobody had done it. Yet it had been done.

On Monday there was a crash of a different sort. After school, Yoko came over and knocked on the back door. Darby swelled with pleasure.

Yoko had never come over before. Darby ran to open the door.

"We're moving," Yoko blurted. One enormous tear slid down the smooth, tawny cheek. Yoko motioned for Darby to come out.

"Moving? But you've lived here all your life." Darby closed the door behind her, and they headed for the woods.

"They're making us move."

"Oh. That's what happened to us. Daddy was transferred. I hate that word, transferred."

"No, no, we're not transferred. Daddy works for himself. He wouldn't transfer himself." Darby knew that Mr. Sasaki was a photographer, but she had never even wondered where he worked. "They're making us move."

"Who?"

"The government. Because we're Japanese."

Darby frowned. That's what one of the kids had said the other day. "That doesn't make one bit of sense."

Yoko shrugged. "I'm not even Japanese," she said. "Everyone of Japanese background has to move. Most of them have already moved. There are lots and lots from California, and they've had to move to camps with just one room for whole families!"

Darby kept the frown on her face, and Yoko

kept her shoulders hunched. "That doesn't make one bit of sense," Darby repeated.

"Daddy's known for a long time. We have to move to some hot place in Florida. At least we'll get to live in a regular house, because we're the only ones from around here. Those camps are awful." Yoko winced. "You can't even go anywhere. There are tall fences to keep everyone inside. With barbed wire on top."

"I don't believe it," Darby said. "I just don't believe it. President Roosevelt wouldn't allow it!" They were standing in the thin woods, not hidden from anything, but Darby shuddered and looked around to be sure she was not surrounded by barbed wire.

"It's true," Yoko wailed. "Daddy's known for a long time, but he just told me. We're moving Friday."

"Friday! Yoko-o-o," Darby wailed, and reached out for Yoko's hands, but they did not twirl "washing machines" as she and Fancy had done. How could Yoko move when they had just started being friends again, when someone had purposely caused her an accident? Just when she was feeling rich with friends she was losing them all again. All but Fancy. "I don't believe it," she repeated. Wasn't this the land of the free? It was too hard to believe such things as Yoko was telling her.

"Ask your father," Yoko said. "Daddy says it's been in the news since the first of the war. Your daddy will know all about it. Just ask him."

With deep regret, Darby recalled her own reaction to finding out that Yoko was Japanese. What if America were at war with Ireland, as Yoko had suggested to help her understand. Would Grandma Mimmie tear up all her Irish linens? Would people of Irish background have to move into camps with fences around them?

The girls wandered over to Yoko's and sat, melancholy, in the swing. Their normal chatter was subdued to nothing. They trailed through the house and came out with a halved lemon and the salt shaker, and they climbed up into the sycamore tree. Muffin clambered up behind them and stretched out dolefully along one limb, head on paws, whining occasionally. Just like Blackie Dog, Muffin knew.

Darby reached out and rubbed Muffin's head. "Don't run away, Muffin. You have to go with Yoko." They stared into space, studied the terra cotta roof on Yoko's house, and gazed off across other rooftops.

"I won't see the sycamore fruit again," Yoko said, and somehow that seemed the saddest thing of all.

When Darby asked her father, hoping, hoping, hoping for a denial, he said it was true.

"Why?" she asked. "Why would people hate someone just because of where their ancestors came from?"

Dad shook his head. "I don't know," he said. "I don't understand hatred myself." He tried to explain to her that people were afraid of anything or anyone different. She thought she should be able to understand this because she'd been thinking about it a lot lately. She had straightened things out for herself, about Yoko and Mr. Kaigler, and here was all this confusion again.

"Yoko's father is a photographer and they're afraid he might photograph something secret at Fort McPherson or at Lockheed, where they build planes. They can't tell who may and who may not be spies, so they're gathering them all." Chills ran through her at the thought of whole groups of people being gathered up because a few were under suspicion. "It's a cruel, cruel thing," Dad said.

"Why doesn't President Roosevelt stop it?" she asked. "He is the president and they couldn't do it if he said not to, could they?"

"That's right, lamb."

"What do you mean?"

"Just what you said. They couldn't do it if he said not to."

"You mean he allows them to do it?"

Dad said something about protecting the country, but how could she understand such things? She ignored Kyla's claim on the bedroom and climbed up to her bunk, where she lay, staring at the ceiling. At dinner, she could hardly eat for the tightness in her throat. After dark, she took her President Roosevelt medallion, which was like a huge coin, and her rabbit's foot, and buried them in her bottom drawer. There was no such thing as good luck.

» 24 «

AT PERKERSON SCHOOL there were no Japanese, so no one there was concerned about what she had learned was called "the removal." When she mentioned it quietly to Fancy and LeRoy on Tuesday, they acted as if they thought it was the right thing to do, even when she tried to explain about the Irish.

Darby resented the world's going right along with daily business. In her Bible readings she had just read about the crucifixion. This war, she thought, was like the crucifixion of the world. She was distressed that the world did not turn black in midafternoon.

In class, they had begun the study of the states and were each making a scrapbook. Today, Darby did California. She drew a camp with a barbed-wire fence all around and Japanese-Americans—Yoko, Kiyo, Mr. and Mrs. Sasaki—holding on to the fence, looking out.

At recess Fancy said, "Spend the night with me Saturday night and go to church with me Sunday morning." Darby had been waiting for this invitation. She had never spent the night anywhere except at home or with Mimmie. She ought to have been excited just thinking about it, but her heart was too heavy to hold excitement.

Fancy, however, was excited enough for both of them. "I've never been allowed to have anyone spend the night before," she said, almost jumping.

"I'll ask," Darby said. They had just mended the friendship and she thought she shouldn't say anything sassy to Fancy about her attitude toward the Japanese-Americans. Fancy was her only friend again. How could she be friends with Valerie and Jim and Sonny if they were friends with Gordon and John? Although she had no proof, she was almost certain that Gordon and John had planned her accident together.

"Of course you can go. But I must say, you don't act any too happy about it," Mother said when she asked. "If it makes you that unhappy, I'll say you can't go."

"I want to go," Darby said with a shrug. "It's just that I'm so sad for Yoko." How could she be mad at Fancy for feeling the very same way that she herself had felt at first?

Every afternoon she stayed with Yoko until suppertime, sitting in the swing or in the sycamore tree. Sometimes eating lemons, sometimes not. Sometimes talking, sometimes not. They made bold plans for what they would do when they were grown up.

"I'll be a scientist, like Madame Curie," Yoko said.

"And I'll be president of the United States, and I won't let things like this happen," said Darby.

After school on Friday, Darby stood in the Sasakis' front yard watching the movers load the last of the furniture. Darby and Yoko pledged to write to each other.

"I mean really," Darby said. "And you'll have to write first to send me your address." Yoko promised.

"We're lucky, really," Yoko said. "At least we get to take our own things. And rent out our house instead of sell it. We'll be back when the war is over. Most people can only take what they can carry on their backs or in their car, because there isn't room in the camps." Darby wanted to cover her ears. She did not want to listen to any more of the awful things that were happening in her own country.

"Here, I have something for you," Yoko said, and she held out a picture.

"For me?" Salt water dashed her eyes as she looked at the picture of the two of them in the sycamore tree.

"To remember me by," Yoko said. It was one of

the pictures Mr. Sasaki had taken that long-ago day when he'd boosted Kiyo and the panda bear up into the tree with Yoko and Darby.

"I'll never forget you, Yoko. Ever," Darby said.

They walked together to Kaigler's and bought one lemon. Because the Sasakis' knives were packed, they asked Mr. Kaigler to cut it for them.

"Moving, eh, *Blümchen?*" he said, slicing the lemon with one swift stroke of his butcher knife, which he then wiped across his apron. "A sad, sad thing. Never thought I'd see such a thing in this country."

Darby noted that he had called Yoko *Blümchen,* and she was glad for that. It was the first time she'd liked the sound of the strange word. There was a warmth in it she'd never noticed before.

"They let me come here. Let me start my own business. They don't make me move. Why?" Mr. Kaigler said. "Because I don't look different. If I keep my mouth shut, who will know?" With motions of his arms, he shooed them away. "Go eat your lemons. Make your blood thin. You think I got all day to make good-byes?"

❖» 25 «❖

❖» SATURDAY. Yoko was gone and the whole world seemed empty. Darby sat on the front steps, because she couldn't bear to go out back and see the white house.

"I've hardly seen you all week," Valerie said, coming over, casually shuffling across the winter brown grass. "It's movie day. It's a Roy Rogers movie."

Going to the movies was like celebrating, and Darby certainly didn't want to celebrate. But how could she miss a Roy Rogers movie? Roy Rogers could possibly be some comfort. "Maybe I'll see you there," she said, unable to be unfriendly to Valerie.

"It's because of the accident, isn't it?" Valerie asked.

"Well, no, but it could be. I mean, I can't be friends with people who are dangerous."

181

"I know what you think, and it wasn't Gordon," Valerie said.

Darby knew that Valerie was just defending Gordon because he was her brother. She'd do the same, she guessed, if anyone accused Kyla of anything. "Then who was it?" Darby asked.

"Well, who wants to see an old Roy Rogers movie, anyway," Valerie said, turning to go. "Hopalong Cassidy is better."

"Is not."

"Is too."

"Is not."

"Is too. What kind of person would name his horse Trigger?"

"What kind of person would name himself Hopalong?"

"Roy Rogers has crinkly eyes."

"Hopalong Cassidy is too old."

When Darby saw the hateful look in Valerie's eyes, she realized there was probably a hateful look in her own. She had already lost Yoko. Somehow, she would have to manage to be friends with Valerie without being friends with the others. "I tell you what," she said. "You like who you like best and I'll like who I like best."

"Okay," Valerie said, "but Hopalong's better."

Darby let Valerie's last remark go. It took effort, sometimes, to be friends.

Later, Darby walked alone to the movies and sat

right smack in the middle of the middle section.
To her surprise and pleasure, Valerie came and
sat with her. Roy Rogers was, if possible, even
more fabulous than he'd been the week before.

When she came home from the movies, Darby
saw a monster moving van at Yoko's. "That is not
your house," she wanted to stomp and shout.
When she left for Fancy's with her gown in the
little snakeskin satchel that Mimmie had given her,
she didn't look at the moving van. She didn't want
to see the people or to know them or know anything about them. No one could take Yoko's place.

She skittered down the bank past the little house
she had called a playhouse. How embarrassed
Fancy must have been. There were certainly a lot
of times when she had been a dumbo about things.

"Come, look," Fancy said, running to meet her
and practically dragging her into the house. Mr.
Potter had made a special effort to finish Fancy's
bedroom for this weekend. It was fantastic. Everything in the room was new, and it all seemed to
have been designed to fit the Sunday Fancy with
the curly hair and the frilly dress. The room was
pink like cotton candy, and the bed had a canopy.

"Oh, Fancy, it's gorgeous," Darby said, falling
backward onto the bed and lying with her arms
outstretched. Sad feelings about Yoko were erased
in the wonder of the room.

At bath time, because the bathtub hadn't yet

been installed, Mrs. Potter filled a washtub from the kitchen sink. Darby felt like a pioneer, with her knees scrunched up to her chin, soaping and rinsing. Fancy bathed next, and then Mrs. Potter changed the water for the little boys.

Afterward, at the kitchen sink, Mrs. Potter helped shampoo Fancy's hair. With a towel wrapped turban-style around her head, Fancy looked as glamorous as she had with curls. Now Mrs. Potter began the process of reproducing those curls. Darby watched in fascination as Fancy's hair was wound into circles and fastened with bobby pins. When the last pin was in place, Fancy jumped up and ran down the hall to her bedroom.

Bundled together in the same bed, they laughed and talked long after the lights went out. Darby remembered that she and Kyla used to lie talking after they had gone to bed.

In the morning, the second phase of the fixing of Fancy's hair began. It was just as interesting as the first. Fancy herself took out the pins, and as she brushed her hair, Darby thought of a butterfly unfolding. How would I look, Darby wondered? Maybe next week she would let Mother do her hair.

At Sunday school, they heard the longest, most boring prayers, as tedious as all the begats in the

Bible. If she were God, Darby thought, she'd appreciate some interesting conversation for a change.

After Sunday school, they walked straight down the aisle of the church and sat on the front pew.

"The preacher makes us sit up front," Fancy said.

"How can he?" Darby asked. "What would he do if we sat back there?" She turned and looked back, realizing that the only thing she didn't like about sitting up front was that she couldn't look around. Many Sundays she had amused herself by examining the people or some of the details of the building.

"He'd say, 'You young people come on up front here,' and he'd wait until we came," Fancy said. "One time his own son sat down in the back and the preacher made him come up front. His shoes squeaked with every step he took."

The organist came in and started playing the music. Everyone sang and then said more long prayers. After the announcements and the offering, Darby settled down to listen to the sermon. The minister started right off shouting, which nearly startled Darby out of the pew. Her Methodist minister was more of a talker. He never raised his voice and only occasionally lifted a hand to gesture. This preacher stomped back and forth on the podium, waving the Bible, which he held open in his hand. Standing right in front of Darby and shaking his Bible as if at her, he shouted, "Repent! Or suffer the everlasting damnation of hell!"

The words shattered her, and she looked around to see if everyone was staring at her. Repent? What did that mean? She certainly knew what *everlasting* and *damnation* and *hell* meant. Now she'd better find out what it was to repent so she could do it.

The longer the minister preached, the more he stomped. Sometimes he lowered his voice so she could barely hear, and just as she began to relax he hollered again or slapped his hand or the Bible against the pulpit.

Putting her hands to her head, Darby checked for horns, to see if she had become a devil. The floor, she thought, would open up any minute and drop her to the fiery pits of hell. She drew her feet onto the pew and sat as she had in the tub last night, all gathered together. Was this what it meant to fear God? It was worse than standing under thirteen trestles. But it was, at least, a proper howling reaction to Yoko's leaving.

❖» 26 «❖

❖» YOKO WAS GONE, but Darby still had to deal with other things in her life. If she refused to be friends with everyone who was hateful about the Japanese, she would have no friends, not even Fancy. And there was still the matter of who had chained the cart to the platform. Inside herself, she examined the neighborhood children with narrow, suspicious eyes.

"I know you think I did it," Gordon said a couple of times. "But I didn't."

"I know you think he did it," Valerie said, "but I know he didn't."

At Sunday school she had quit earning points for her team. She had missed two Sundays, the first because of the accident and the second because she'd gone to church with Fancy. On the third Sunday, when asked about her readings, she

187

just pressed her lips together and shook her head.
The people on her team nearly fainted.

Darby was keeping up with her Bible reading
schedule and even learning her memory verses,
but she still stung from the cross examination on
Obadiah. She had decided that Sunday to read the
Bible only for herself. She would no longer read
for points.

There were still friendly times with Fancy at
school, and walking with her after school. At the
Stewart Avenue corner they often saw LeRoy
sweeping the barber shop or, more often, standing
out front leaning on the broom to look important
as his schoolmates passed by.

"Hey," she said to Fancy one day. "I'll bet I
could get a job sweeping at Kaigler's." Her mind
sprang into action. If she had a job it would oc-
cupy her time, as well as provide her with extra
money.

"You mean that spy store?" Fancy said.

Darby looked surprised. If word of Mr. Kaigler's being a spy had spread this far, perhaps it was
true. She cut off the thought, ashamed of herself.

As soon as she had reported in at home she
started over to Kaigler's. As she crossed the woods
she heard the door bang from over at Yoko's. A
girl about her own age came down the front steps
and headed up the sidewalk toward the store.
Darby slowed her step and wandered circles in the

woods. Resentment flooded her. She didn't want
another girl in Yoko's house, walking across
Yoko's porch, climbing in Yoko's sycamore tree.
She also resented herself for waiting in the woods,
like Gordon and the others, for "city people" to
come out of the store before she went in.

The man with Greta came out of the store and
waved to her. Darby waved back. Gordon and Jim
and John were playing idly at the corner. She
knew they were waiting to follow him. For weeks
she'd watched them follow him everywhere, which
meant back and forth to Kaigler's or elsewhere
around the neighborhood. They hadn't mentioned knowing that the great white dog had had
puppies, and she hadn't told them.

Several city children came down the sidewalk
from the other direction just as the new girl
emerged from the store. When they passed her on
their way into the store, they shouted:

"Freak."

"Holy roller."

"Witch."

Now what? Darby wondered. It was city kids calling a city kid names. Just because she was new
here? It was a chilly day instead of a hot one, but
Darby vividly remembered being in her place in
that very doorway, and how the heat from the
sidewalk had risen and turned her face red. The
emptiness of that day reached out and wrapped

around her again, all these months later. Without thinking, she walked out of the woods and met the girl on the corner.

"Hi, I'm Darby Bannister," Darby said. "I heard them talking mean to you. They did the same thing to me when I first moved here. Don't pay any attention."

The girl shrugged. "I'm Jeannine Flynn. I told them at school that the world was coming to an end soon and they don't believe me." Darby looked at the girl to see if she was teasing.

"The end of the world? Says who?" she asked, trying not to reveal how interested she was. Why, it was almost as though she'd been thinking it herself without realizing it.

"These are the last days," the girl said. "The Bible says so."

"Where does it say that?" Darby was disappointed. She wanted a real prophecy. She had just about finished reading the whole Bible and she hadn't seen anything about the world ending at a certain time. In fact, she remembered something about no one knowing the day or the hour.

Jeannine quoted some scriptures, something about only a certain number of people, one hundred and forty-four thousand, entering into heaven.

"I'd be interested to know more about it," Darby said. "Maybe one day I'll come over and we can sit

up in the sycamore tree and talk about it. Yoko—
she's the girl who used to live there—and I used to
do that. Sit up in the tree and talk about things."
But there would be no more curling up in the
basket swing. The basket swing had gone with
Yoko to "some hot place in Florida."

"I'd like that," the girl said. "But we'd better do
it soon, because it's ending a week from Sunday."

"You mean you even know the exact day?"
Darby was engrossed. The end of the world would
give meaning to the things that had been happening lately. She wanted to believe it. She was ready
for the glory of the end of the world.

With her mind filled and spilling over, she went
to Kaigler's to ask about a job. Mr. Kaigler was
waiting on someone at the counter, a young man
who was ready to pay for some purchases.

"I see we finally got rid of that Jap family," the
young man was saying, holding some dollar bills
toward Mr. Kaigler. Darby stopped as though her
feet had suddenly been nailed to the floor.

"You will not say such things in this store," Mr.
Kaigler said, his hand reaching for the money.

"Says who?" the young man said. Darby gasped
for breath.

"Says Kaigler whose store this is, that's who."
Mr. Kaigler withdrew his hand and gripped the
edge of the counter. But his voice was neither
more nor less gruff than usual.

"I should have known you were a Jap lover," the guy said, still holding out his money and looking around at Darby. "Your customers are Jap lovers."

"I am a human being lover," Mr. Kaigler said. "I will keep my groceries, and you will keep your money."

The young man looked at the money in his hand, then looked at Mr. Kaigler. "Are you saying that you won't sell me these groceries?"

"I am saying," Mr. Kaigler said, "get out of my store." The silence nearly exploded as Mr. Kaigler and the young man stared at each other. Darby remained still and silent, rooted to her spot. She noticed Mrs. Kaigler standing in the doorway behind the meat cases, as tense and motionless as Mother had been when Darby had asked Daddy about the heathen.

"Fine," the young man said quietly. "You keep your groceries. You keep all of your groceries. When word gets around, no one will shop in your store." He ground his heel against the floor, spun around, and stalked out with long stomping steps.

When the door closed behind him, Darby was suddenly free again. She hurried up to the counter, where Mr. Kaigler had already begun gathering what were to have been the young man's groceries.

"Can he do that?" she said.

"What? Stop people from shopping here? Nah. The door is open. People come in if they want to come in. And what for you today, *Blümchen?*" She wanted to tell him how sorry she was about what had happened. She wanted to thank him for defending Yoko's family. But her mind clattered with anger and hurt and her tongue would not say the words.

"Yeh, yeh, take your time," he said, when he saw her confusion. Arms loaded, he walked around the store and began to replace the goods on the shelves.

Now was certainly not the time to ask him about a job, she thought. But she'd worked up her courage to ask, and in spite of what had just taken place, she decided to go ahead. Now or never, she thought.

"I was wondering," she said when he returned, "if you needed somebody to sweep your store?"

"Sweep the store? I shave in the morning and I sweep the store in the evening. Both automatic. I do it without thinking. Why should I need someone else to do it? Eh?"

Sorry she'd asked, she shrugged, muttered something feeble, and bought two cents' worth of licorice stars.

In her Bible readings that night, Darby suddenly found the passage about the one hundred and forty-four thousand Jeannine had said would enter into heaven. It was in the seventh chapter of Revelation verse four. Twelve thousand from each of the twelve tribes of Israel would be saved. To read it tonight, the same day she'd first heard about it, was surely a sign, she thought. Besides, with wars and removals and maybe even spies, this was certainly an end-of-the-world time. Darby firmly believed that the world was going to end soon. Jeannine said it would end in less than two weeks. Sunday after next.

In bed, she thought about the end of the world. Would it be frightening, like an earthquake cracking the world open to expose the fires of hell? She remembered how terrified she'd been, sitting on the front row of Fancy's church. But the faithful should be joyful, not frightened. She didn't know which of the twelve tribes she was from, but she knew she was among them.

"Kyla, do you ever think of the end of the world?" she said quietly in the dark, guarding herself against the "dumbo" that was sure to come.

"It ended the day we moved," Kyla said from below.

"No, I mean really," Darby said.

"No," Kyla said.

"What would you do if it was soon? What if you knew for certain that it was going to end, say, a

week from Sunday?" Eyes open, she stared at the
ceiling in the dark, playing out her visions on it
just as she did on the cloth front of the radio.

"It couldn't be too soon for me," Kyla said.

Suddenly irritated, Darby blurted, "Oh, go
drown yourself in your own misery."

"I will," Kyla said.

"You're so busy feeling sorry for yourself that a
person can't even have a decent conversation with
you. I'm sick and tired of it." Then there was silence.

In a minute Darby heard Kyla sniffing, like she
had a cold. She's crying, Darby thought. Well,
good enough for her.

In another minute Kyla's misery had overcome
Darby with sympathy. With repentence. She had
looked up the word *repent.* What it meant was to
be sorry and not to do something anymore. And
she was sorry. She was sorry for Kyla's misery and
sorry that Kyla didn't have any friends and sorry
that she had been unsympathetic. She would be
kinder to Kyla, more understanding, from now on
until the end of the world—which wouldn't be
long.

After school the next day, she went to Kaigler's
to buy a lemon.

"Eh, *Blümchen,* are you still interested in sweeping my store?"

With the excitement over the end of the world, she had forgotten about wanting a job. A job would no longer be necessary.

"I was upset the other day," Mr. Kaigler said. He made shooing motions, as if he were trying to rid the store of the memory of what had happened. "I wasn't thinking. I do need someone to sweep the front walk twice a day. If you can come over before school and just before six in the afternoons, I'll pay you twenty-five cents a week. Do you want the job?"

Twenty-five cents a week. Her heart leaped. In two weeks she could buy a new box of stationery. In another week, she'd have enough for six stamps, as well. But what good would that do if the world was ending? Though what if it didn't? No. She erased her doubts. She would be watching and found faithful. Still, she had asked for the job in the first place and it would be rude to say no.

"Yes," she said, excitement invading her in spite of everything. "Just wait until I tell Mother and Dad!" She whirled and ran for the door.

"One minute, *Blümchen*," he said. "Did you come in for something, or are you carrying that nickel around to feel rich?"

She bought the lemon and hurried home to halve it and to tell Mother about her job.

"My, such excitement," Mother said when Darby told her.

"Yes, and the end of the world, too," she said, grabbing the salt shaker and reaching for the back door.

"What?" Mother said, but Darby was already leaping across the door sill and down all three stairs at once, and she didn't hear Mother's question.

With the lemon and salt shaker in one hand, she knocked at Jeannine's door with the other. "Is Jeannine here?" she asked the woman who came to the door.

"You must be Darby," the woman said.

"Yes," Darby said, realizing immediately that she had not added *ma'am*. Jeannine's mother did not seem to notice.

"I think Jeannine's out back with the dog." Darby walked through the yard feeling a little shy, the edge gone from her excitement. It was strange not to have Yoko here. When she saw the dog, she blinked. The dog looked just like Muffin.

"Is that your dog?" she asked, wondering if Muffin had leaped out of the Sasakis' car, determined to stay "home," like Blackie Dog.

"Yes, this is Duchess," Jeannine said, answering Darby from her spot up in the tree. "Come on up."

The dog scrambled up the tree. Shyly and uncertainly, Darby followed. When she reached Jeannine, she held out half a lemon.

"Yoko and I used to sit up here and eat lemons. Want one?"

Jeannine made a face. "Aren't they sour?"

"Mmmm. Sour but good," Darby said, salting both halves and handing one to Jeannine.

"I know it's hard to move," Darby said. "Things are always so strange at first."

"Well, I didn't move all that far, but I had to change schools. I didn't like the other school all that much, but at least they were used to my ways."

Darby settled snugly on a limb and dug her teeth into the lemon. "You mean about the end of the world?"

"Well, yeah. And other stuff."

"What other stuff?" Darby was anxious to hear about some different things.

"Like not saluting the flag."

Darby sat up so suddenly that she almost toppled out of the tree. Duchess barked at her. "You mean you don't salute the flag?" Perhaps she didn't want to hear about different things after all. Perhaps she had heard about more strange things than she wanted to already. How weird the world was.

"We pledge our allegiance only to God," Jeannine said.

That sounded so reasonable, so sensible, that

Darby found herself nodding in understanding, if not agreement. But then, everyone else saluted the flag and pledged themselves to God, too.

Jeannine added: "Saluting the flag is a symbol of obedience to the government, and we obey no authority but God."

Confusion flew about inside Darby's head. "Don't you buy savings stamps and save string and tin cans?"

Jeannine shook her head. "We don't support war."

So many new things were being revealed to Darby. She didn't support war, either. Nobody supported war. But the Japanese had attacked. What were people to do if they were attacked? She had never known there were so many ways of believing. How was she to know which was right?

As soon as they had said the blessing that night, and Daddy had started to serve the food, Mother said, "What's this end-of-the-world business?"

Kyla rolled her eyes. "She started that the other night."

"Jeannine says that the world is going to end a week from Sunday," Darby said. She knew by their expressions that she had already said too much. Jeannine said it did no good to try to tell unbelievers about the end of the world. But her family were believers, except maybe for Dad.

"And on what basis does she say this?" Dad asked.

"She says it's in the Bible," Darby said, and she repeated some of the things Jeannine had told her. It was all right to tell her family. In fact, she had the responsibility to tell her family.

"And you believe it, of course," said Kyla.

"I saw about the one hundred forty-four thousand myself. Twelve thousand of each of the twelve tribes of Israel."

"That sort of leaves you out," Kyla said, "since you're not from Israel."

"No one's from Israel anymore," Dad said. "At least not geographically. There is no country Israel." Darby forked mashed potatoes into her mouth, then string beans.

"So only God knows who the twelve tribes are anymore," Darby said.

"Darby, don't talk with your mouth full," Blair said.

"I told you she believed it," Kyla said.

"No, I don't, really," Darby said, begging forgiveness for the lie even as she said it. She didn't tell about not saluting the flag. Perhaps she would ask Dad about it sometime. If the world was going to end, it wouldn't matter.

Then Mother came at Darby with the "knoweth no man" passage. " 'But of that day and that hour knoweth no man, no, not the angels which are in heaven, neither the Son, but the Father. Take ye heed, watch and pray: for ye know not when the time is.' "

"So, then, it could be," Darby said, "if no one knows."

"It could be," Dad conceded, "but I very much doubt it."

"There have always been false prophets," Mother said.

"You have to be careful whom you let influence you," Dad said. "What you have to do is learn as much as you can about everything and then decide for yourself."

"But there are signs," Darby said.

"What signs?" snapped Kyla.

"What signs?" said Dad seriously. At least he discussed things reasonably.

"Wars," she said, and then muffled herself with food.

"And don't forget pestilence," Kyla said.

Mother and Dad glanced at each other from opposite ends of the table, Mother concerned, Daddy amused. What if it really was the end of the world and her family wasn't watching and praying? The very thought almost made her cry.

After dinner, without letting Kyla see her, Darby looked up *pestilence*.

"A fatal epidemic disease." Polio! She was all the more certain that the prophecy was true.

In the morning, Darby began her job at Kaigler's. Sweeping the walk was the easiest thing in the world, and she seemed to finish too quickly, but she did have to get along to school. That evening there were a few candy wrappers and one cigarette package to throw in the trash. She lingered over the broom.

"This is a two-cent job, *Blümchen,*" Mr. Kaigler said from the doorway. "I'm not paying you a nickel for a two-cent job, just because you take a nickel's worth of time doing it."

By Saturday, she was eagerly looking forward to being paid. Sweeping twice a day for six days at two cents a sweep, with a penny extra for a full week's work, would bring her twenty-five cents. For Wednesday through Saturday, she would get sixteen cents. But after this week, she would have enough on Saturdays to pay for her own movie, buy five cents' worth of licorice stars, and have eleven cents left over. Immediately she chastised herself for planning ahead when there would be no future.

That afternoon, as she walked down Deckner to the movie, Darby felt very alone. Every once in a while she turned and looked back, not knowing whether the neighborhood people were ahead of or behind her. Perhaps Valerie would sit with her again. When she turned the corner onto Dill, she saw them all, standing in front of the theater.

"Oh, I was hoping you'd come," Valerie said, running toward her, quickly grasping her hand and just as quickly dropping it. That was a lot for Valerie to show in front of Gordon. "You're still going to be friends, aren't you?"

Darby winced. There was no easy way to be friends with Valerie and not be friends with the others. She could have been crippled for life, and she could not forget it that easily. Nevertheless, she stood behind Valerie in the ticket line. After today, there would be only one more Saturday movie before the end of the world. The thought was both disturbing and delicious.

Sucking on the first licorice star, she entered the theater. Valerie followed her to a seat in the middle section. The theater darkened, and Roy Rogers and Trigger began to gallop across the screen. At least she'd had the chance to know Roy Rogers before the end.

After the movie, Darby went home and tried to ignore her former friends as they romped through the neighborhood in their weekly reenactment. She had her job, and that would be enough. Later, as she swept in front of Kaigler's, she wished they would come by. She would lean casually on the broom, as LeRoy did. Some city kids appeared across the street, but they didn't count. She didn't know them and she doubted that they would be impressed by her job. She just kept on sweeping.

All of a sudden Darby was attacked. "Jap lover. Traitor. Spy. Working at a Jap-lover spy store!" At first, she just looked up in surprise. Then, as a rain of pebbles pelted her, she held the broom over her head for protection. The stones dashed the sidewalk, rang against the window, and stung her legs before the shouting, sneering children stampeded down the street.

Mr. Kaigler was there in a second. *"Blümchen, are you all right?"* He stooped, first, to check her legs, then balled his fist, raised his arm, and shook it after the disappearing herd of children.

"No, I'm not hurt," she said, looking at a red dot where a pebble had struck the meaty part of her calf.

"Pigs! Fascist pigs!" Mr. Kaigler shouted, and he spat on the freshly-swept sidewalk.

» 27 «

BEFORE SCHOOL on Monday, Darby bounded around to Kaigler's, shoved against the door and, to her surprise, felt pushed back. The door had not opened. Again she pushed. It still did not yield. Shielding her eyes from the glare of the glass, she peered inside. Everything seemed normal, except that Mr. Kaigler always opened at seven, and it was past seven-thirty.

Had they made him close his store for being a Jap lover? Had he been arrested for being a spy? Had they forced him to move, as they had Yoko? She was partly to blame. If only she, whom they also called Jap lover, had not started sweeping Kaigler's sidewalk, maybe this would not have happened.

Darby ran home in alarm.

"He's probably on vacation," Dad said.

"But I work there," she said. "He wouldn't go off on vacation without telling me he was going."

"They must have had an emergency," Mother said. "I hope it isn't too serious." Darby had not told them about the stone-throwing, name-calling incident because she was afraid they would make her quit her job. But now she told them everything, even about the young man in the store and what the kids had said about Mr. Kaigler.

"They threw stones at *you?*" Mother said.

"Who threw stones at you?" Dad said. Both of them hovered as though it had just happened. Darby's response to their reaction was tears, and Dad pulled her to him, hugging and patting. "Okay, lamb. It's all right. It's all right."

"But Mr. Kaigler," Darby said, snuffling.

"Just calm down, lamb," Dad said. "I'm sure everything you say is true, but I'm just as sure there's a reasonable explanation for Mr. Kaigler's absence, and we'll find it out in due time. I don't think Mr. Kaigler was taken away against his will."

"But the Sasakis were," she said. To this he had no answer.

With the assurance of one having superior knowledge, Gordon told everyone at school about Mr. Kaigler's disappearance.

"I told you he was a spy," he said to Darby.

"Shut up," she said to him.

After school she walked directly to Kaigler's,

fantasizing that the store would be open and that she would get right to work. There was a gang of kids in front of the store, including Gordon, Valerie, Jim, John, and Sonny.

"We got rid of the Japs," one of the children was saying. "And now we got rid of one Jap lover."

"Well, you're not getting rid of me," Darby said. "And I liked him." She visualized Mr. Kaigler's bushy hair and craggy face, with the smile that was just like another wrinkle.

"You would, you Yankee Jap lover," one of them said.

"Sticks and stones may break my bones, but names will never hurt me," she said, and she raised her chin like she was the Queen of the World. Of course, it was totally untrue that names would never hurt her. Sometimes words stung like wasps. "You talk about mean old Mr. Kaigler, well, I think y'all are the mean ones." The *y'all* slipped out so naturally it surprised her. "I don't think he's a spy, and I happen to know that he's just on vacation." With her head held high, she turned and walked away. Their laughter broke like a storm at her back.

"Vacation."

"Ha, ha."

"Where did he go on vacation, Miss Know-it-all?"

As gracefully as she could, Darby turned only

her head and said, "Florida." Then she walked regally across the street and through the woods.

She hoped he was on vacation. She hoped that more than she hoped an emergency was what had taken him away. Though she would have preferred an emergency to what she really thought— that because some people believed Mr. Kaigler was a spy, he'd been taken away.

Before she reached her yard, she saw Jeannine standing on the porch. She swerved left and crossed Stewart. "How come you're not over in front of Kaigler's?" she said, as she trailed Jeannine around back to the tree. "Everyone else is."

"I'm not everyone else," Jeannine said. "They are of the world."

"Huh?"

"We are to be in the world, but not of the world," Jeannine said. " 'Love not the world, neither the things that are in the world. If any man love the world, the love of the Father is not in him.' First John two, fifteen."

"Yes, I read that," Darby said. "It didn't make any sense, so I didn't pay much attention to it." She swung herself up to a higher limb than usual.

"You can't just choose the parts you like," Jeannine said from below her. Darby recalled that Yoko had said the same thing.

"But I love the world," Darby said, "and the

things of the world." Then she thought of the crowd of kids in front of Kaigler's. "At least, some of the things of the world." She looked up through the sycamore tree with its bare branches holding up the sky. "If He made the world, if He created it, He must love it and want us to love it, too."

"Well, He's ending it. That's how much He loves it," Jeannine said, which brought Darby's thoughts back to Mr. Kaigler.

"What do you think about Mr. Kaigler?" she asked.

"I don't even think about Mr. Kaigler," Jeannine said.

"Well, you're the only one, then," Darby said. "Doesn't that make you lukewarm?" She felt proud to have a Biblical comeback. " 'Because thou art lukewarm, and neither cold nor hot, I will spew thee out of my mouth.' Revelation three, sixteen." It was a verse she had memorized just for herself and was one of her favorites in the whole Bible. She herself was most often hot, and sometimes cold, but very seldom lukewarm.

"But Mr. Kaigler is of the world."

"He might not be anymore." Darby recoiled from the thought. What did they do with spies? And where was Mrs. Kaigler? Was she a spy, too? If not, what had they done with her? Had they made her leave, too, just as Yoko had had to leave because of her father?

"Can you come over Sunday?" Jeannine asked.

"Sunday. Isn't that the day? Don't you think I should stay with my family?"

"Do they believe it?"

"Uh . . . well . . ."

"That's what I thought. So will you be able to watch and pray without them being upset with you? Mother says it doesn't matter where we are, as long as we are faithful. I thought I'd like to sit up here and see what direction the end comes from first."

"Won't it come from all around at once?"

Jeannine hunched her shoulders. "If it does, we can see it all around at once from here."

Darby looked around. Sure enough, she could see Kaigler's and her own house and halfway down Stewart.

"What if it boils up from hell?" Darby asked. She shuddered, thinking that Fancy's preacher could cause the end of the world all by himself.

"However it happens," Jeannine said, "the righteous shall be gathered unto Him."

Darby pictured herself right here in the sycamore tree, being faithful and keeping watch. She could see Him coming, arms extended to gather them in, with His white robe filling half the sky.

She felt like a holy prophet who would be among the first to be gathered. She hoped He would recognize her as Queen of the World.

With the end of the world practically in sight, Darby thought she should do something special, rather than simply wait. There was nothing she could do for Mr. Kaigler, whether he was a spy or not. Nor could she do anything for Yoko, whose spirit filled her heart. All she could do, she decided, was to be kind to Kyla, and try to remember to say *ma'am* to Miss Hardy.

That night she reread the third chapter of Revelation, where it said, "Because thou art lukewarm, and neither cold nor hot, I will spew thee out of my mouth." She smiled with the sure knowledge that, whatever she was, she was not lukewarm. She was hot and getting hotter. There was no fear left in her, only joy and excitement at the thought of being alive to witness the final glory.

❖ » 28 « ❖

❖» EVERY DAY Darby walked over to Kaigler's,
hoping the store would be open and Mr.
Kaigler would be there with his butcher apron on,
just like always. One day she took Mother's broom
and swept the sidewalk, steeling herself against
stones and jeers. But there were none. She remained all alone, sweeping the sidewalk.

On Friday, the day of the last spelling test of the
world, LeRoy wore new shoes to school. Since he
quit going barefooted, he'd been wearing black
high-topped sneakers. Darby wouldn't have partic-
ularly noticed if he hadn't turned sideways in his
desk and stuck his feet practically in her face.

"See my new shoes?" he said, turning his foot
this way and that so she could see the shoes from
every angle. You would think he had a new bicy-
cle, Darby thought.

"Yes, they're very nice," she said politely,

though she didn't know why he thought they were such a big deal. They were just plain brown oxfords, nothing special, like her huaraches would be. What would he say if she told him new shoes were a waste?

"Now I won't have to come to school barefooted this spring," he said.

"I thought you liked to go barefooted," she said. Why else had he run around that way?

"Not to school," he said. "I'd rather wear shoes to school."

Suddenly, Miss Hardy called her name. "Darby, would you like to give out the spelling papers?" Darby rose immediately, glad for any opportunity to be up and out of her desk.

"Yes," she answered quickly, but as soon as she had said it she sensed the emptiness where *ma'am* should have been. Before she could say the unfamiliar word, Miss Hardy cut in.

"You mean, yes, ma'am?"

"Yes, ma'am," Darby said. The word scraped across her tongue and barbed her lips.

"Well, never mind, Darby," Miss Hardy said. "I'll let someone else do it."

Darby faltered in the aisle. Her eyes dropped, falling on LeRoy's shiny brown shoes. She wanted to flee, but she was stuck in this classroom. The end of the world was coming two days too late.

"I dislike having to embarrass you, Darby, but since you persist in your stubbornness, perhaps this will help you remember," Miss Hardy said. The response "Yes, ma'am" popped into Darby's head, but she refused to turn it loose. She plodded the three steps back to her desk.

"You're really going to make her mad one of these days," Fancy said to Darby at recess.

"But I can't help it. I'm not refusing to say it on purpose, no matter what she thinks. Some of the words you use are so strange to me that I just can't remember."

"As smart as you are, you can remember if you want to," Fancy said. "I think you *are* being stubborn. You just say it to yourself. Yes, ma'am, no, ma'am, yes, ma'am, no, ma'am, until it sounds familiar."

The advice made Darby flush with anger, and that made her think maybe she *was* being stubborn. Otherwise, why would she be angry? Sometimes knowing that she was wrong made her angriest of all. It was true, she did not want *ma'am* to become familiar to her. Or *y'all,* or *hey,* or *tote.*

"Did you see LeRoy's new shoes?" she said, to change the subject.

"Aren't they beautiful?" Fancy said.

"What is so great about those shoes?" Darby asked, her irritation over the *ma'am*s spilling over onto LeRoy's shoes. "He practically stuck them in my face. Why did he come barefooted all last fall if he'd rather wear shoes?"

Fancy shook her head and looked disgusted. "How can you be so smart and so dumb at the same time? He didn't wear shoes because he didn't have any. His family can't afford shoes, except for cold weather." Fancy stood with her hands on her hips, yammer-jammering. "Don't you know LeRoy works because he has to buy his own clothes? He bought those shoes from money he earned himself. That's why he's so proud of them. That's why it's such a big deal."

Darby felt like she'd been plunged beneath Niagara Falls. LeRoy's family could not afford shoes? She could scarcely imagine it. There were a lot of things her own family could not afford, but not such everyday things as shoes. If he had wanted shoes enough to work and buy them for himself, then he wanted them more than she wanted huaraches. Except for the huaraches, she had never even wanted shoes. Shoes were just always there, like food.

Darby absorbed the message about being dumb. It wasn't that she had no brain, but that she didn't use her eyes. The Bible said something about "he who has eyes, let him see." Circuits began to connect in her brain. LeRoy–shoes–money–panda. If

LeRoy could earn money to buy his own shoes, she could earn money to buy her own panda. Immediately she remembered that she no longer had a job. And, besides, the world was coming to an end.

At home, a letter addressed to Miss Darby Bannister awaited her. It was the first mail she'd ever received, except for birthday cards from relatives. The letter was typed. "Thank you for your letter and your prayers. The support of people at home is so important to our morale." Her eyes snapped to the signature. Typed across the bottom was "General Dwight D. Eisenhower." But he had signed it "Ike."

Darby jumped up and down, flapping the letter in the air, ready to run and show the world. Then she remembered her vow. This was only for herself and not to be used for boasting. Tucking the letter in the pocket of her dress, she thought, I won't even tell the Boys' Bataan Prayer Band.

As she sat on the front steps, glorying over the letter in her pocket, Valerie came over. Darby clamped her teeth together to keep from telling.

"I've hardly seen you all week," Valerie said. Darby shrugged and moved to the side of the steps to make room for Valerie. How could she blame Valerie for what the others had done? "In fact, I've hardly seen you since—since—"

"The accident," Darby filled in.

"I know what you think," Valerie said, "but it

wasn't Gordon. I keep telling you it wasn't Gordon."

"Who was it then?" She was tired of Valerie's empty defenses of Gordon, even if he was her brother. "Someone wanted to hurt me because I was braver than Gordon."

"Oh, no," Valerie said, "it wasn't like that at all."

"You mean you know who it was? You really do know who it was, don't you?" Valerie twisted the hemline of her skirt. "You'd better tell me," Darby said. "If you ever want us to be friends again, you'd better tell me."

Valerie hesitated. "The one who did it didn't know it would be dangerous," she said. "They just thought the cart wouldn't move when it was pushed. They were really a secret spy, really on Shana's side and trying to help her without the others' knowing."

"How do you know that?" Darby demanded, looking at Valerie, who was looking at her own feet the same way Darby had looked at LeRoy's feet. Her own humiliation washed over her. Was that what Valerie was feeling? And why? "How do you know?" she repeated, as Valerie resumed twisting her hem.

"And the person just nearly died when it turned into an accident and would have died if you'd been hurt, and the person feels just terrible that you won't be friends anymore because you're the

first girl who's lived on the block besides me
and—" Seeing Darby looking at her, Valerie
stopped abruptly, jumped up, and ran.

"Valerie, come back," Darby called out. This was
her day for seeing.

Valerie turned and spat out the words, "It was
me. It was me. And even if we're never friends
again, I'm just glad you weren't hurt."

Darby was on her feet in an instant, running
after Valerie and calling, "It's all right. It's all
right. Please come back. I do want to be friends."

Valerie stopped and walked slowly back to the
steps. "I wanted to tell you. I've been wanting to
tell you, but you were so angry about it. I didn't
think you'd listen to me."

"Did they know?" Darby asked.

"Only Gordon," Valerie said.

Gordon knew? All this time, Gordon knew?

"And he didn't tell?" Darby asked. No, of course
he didn't tell. She would have been the very one to
know if he had told. Now she could be friends
with them, after all. "What's on at the movies tomorrow?" she asked, to let Valerie know that everything was all right.

"Roy Rogers," Valerie said with disappointment.
"That's all they've been showing lately." And they
began discussing the pros and cons of Roy Rogers
and Hopalong Cassidy.

"I wish Yoko were still here," Valerie said after a

while. Darby looked up with interest. "I was never friends with her and I should have been," Valerie said. "I wish we could ask her to come to the movies with us."

"Too bad you never asked before," Darby said, working hard to contain her resentment. What good was it for Valerie to be sorry now?

"Things are different now," Valerie said.

Darby opened her mouth to tell Valerie how really different things were, about how the world was going to end on Sunday, but she stopped. She looked out across the brown winter lawn and down the street of wooden frame houses. Everything looked exactly the same as always. But by Sunday it would all be topsy turvy.

"Now I know how it feels for someone to— uh—not like me," Valerie said. "Maybe we could ask that new girl."

"Jeannine?" Darby asked.

"I don't know her name. The one who moved into Yoko's house."

"That's Jeannine. Do you mean it?" Darby leaped up with delight. "Come on. Let's go ask her."

Valerie hung back. "You go. You're the one who knows her."

Darby didn't argue. "Okay. I'll go right now. If I don't see you later, I'll see you tomorrow, okay? And I'm glad we're friends again." She ran through the thin woods and across the street to Jeannine's. She was thrilled that Valerie wanted Jeannine to go to the movies. It was an apology to Yoko.

"Hi, can you come to the movies with us tomorrow?" Darby asked, when Jeannine came to the door. Going to the movies was a little frivolous if the world was ending, but it was a Roy Rogers movie and Darby didn't want to miss it.

"Movies are of the earth," Jeannine said.

"Holy cow," Darby said. Jeannine needed to cut a hole in the Bible and climb inside it. Darby believed in the Bible. Hadn't she read it all the way through? But she thought she used good sense about it. "But it's a Roy Rogers movie," she said.

"Who's Roy Rogers?" Jeannine asked.

"You don't know who Roy Rogers is?" Darby said, though she'd only known about him herself for a short time. Eagerly she described the handsome singing cowboy to Jeannine, telling about his crinkly eyes and his fantastic horse, Trigger.

"I wish I could go," Jeannine said, catching some of the excitement.

"Well, ask."

Jeannine shook her head, looking a little sad. "Let's get some lemons to eat while we wait for the end of the world," she suggested.

"You mean you're going to eat lemons while you

wait for the world to end?" Darby asked. It was strange, she thought, the way each of them took different things seriously.

"Well, I don't think He'd mean for us to go hungry while we still have our earthly bodies," Jeannine said. "Let's get a dozen!"

Jeannine dashed inside to get some money and then followed Darby home, while Darby got her share. Because Kaigler's was closed, they had to go down across from the drugstore to the new supermarket. Darby had never been inside it before, and was confused by all the aisles and counters.

"Who gets your groceries for you?" Darby asked.

"You get them yourself," Jeannine said, leading the way.

At all the grocery stores Darby had ever been in, you told the grocer what you wanted and he got it for you. Darby longed for Mr. Kaigler to say, "What'll it be today? Eh, *Blümchen?*" The bright lights and slick tile floor made her miss Mr. Kaigler even more. She longed for the comfort of dimness and worn plank floors.

"What keeps people from just walking out with groceries without paying?" Darby said. Jeannine had found her way to the lemons, and they had each picked out six.

"You have to go out through the check-out

counters," Jeannine said, leading Darby back to the front of the store, where they paid for the lemons. No one called them by name or nickname, or wondered aloud what two girls were going to do with a dozen lemons.

"I liked Kaigler's better," Jeannine said, as they pushed through the glass swinging door. Darby smiled in agreement.

"I wonder what will happen to it," Darby said. "Kaigler's store."

"Oh, they'll sell it, or something. Someone else will take over."

"I'll bet he won't be as nice as Mr. Kaigler," Darby said. As they walked along brooding, Darby thought that she really, truly did like Mr. Kaigler, including his gruffness. How could she bear having someone else run that store? She would rather have it stay closed forever. Did Mr. Kaigler know how much she liked him? She had never even thanked him for that orange drink.

At home she asked, "Daddy, what does *Blümchen* mean?"

"Flower, I think. Little flower. Why, lamb?"

"Mr. Kaigler used to call me that," she said, feeling empty inside.

When Darby was ready to go to the movies, she decided that for the first and last time she would buy her refreshments at the theater. They cost more there, but she couldn't stand to go back to the supermarket. At the last minute, she had an idea and acted on impulse, without thinking.

"Kyla, why don't you come with us?"

"With us where?" Kyla asked, though Darby was certain Kyla knew.

"To the movies. It's Roy Rogers."

Kyla sat for a minute, not answering. Darby, used to being ignored, was about to turn away, when Kyla said, "Okay, I might."

Darby held her breath and was careful not to ruin everything by acting amazed. "Well, okay, but come on right now. It's time to go."

To Darby's further surprise, Gordon didn't make any smart remarks about Kyla's presence. He knows I'm Queen of the World, she thought smugly, so he wouldn't dare say anything about my sister. She immediately asked forgiveness for her haughty attitude. There was such a halo on her head she couldn't believe it. She guessed it was because she was prepared for the end.

The next day, the Sunday school contest ended, and the winning team was chosen. Darby's team won. Except for Darby, they were all called to the front of the room to receive a blue ribbon. Darby's eyes burned, even though she tried not to mind. If they were mad at her because she'd stopped trading her reading for points, that was their problem, wasn't it? So what if she didn't get a blue ribbon? Though she'd certainly won enough points to deserve one.

"For one person, we have a special award," the superintendent said. "One person in this department has put forth a special effort and accomplished what most adults have never accomplished. Darby?" She held out a huge double ribbon with a ruffled rosette at the top.

Darby was stunned. Someone pushed her toward the front, and she forced her legs to move. With her chin on her chest, she accepted the ribbon and listened while they praised her.

"I think Darby deserves our appreciation for the example she has set, don't you?" The superintendent began clapping, and the others joined in. "Darby, you may be interested to know that if you had been a team all by yourself, you would still have won this contest." The group cheered and applauded again.

After the applause had died, they all gathered around, begging to see the ribbon. "I don't know how you did it," they exclaimed. Some of them patted her on the back. "We're very proud of you," they all said. And Darby beamed.

❖》 29 《❖

》DARBY RAN HOME from Sunday school to
hang the ribbon on the wall. She squeezed her
hair into two tiny pigtails and tried not to bolt
down her dinner. When she darted across Stewart
and bounded toward the sprawling sycamore tree,
Jeannine was already there with Duchess, the
lemons, a salt shaker, and a knife.

"Has it started yet?" Darby asked, scanning the
horizon and then looking up. There was no black-
ness, no rainbow, and no giant Jesus walking
through the sky with flowing robes. "Is that a
cloud over there?" she asked, straining her eyes to
the southeast over Deckner's fields, toward Lake-
wood Park.

"I don't think so," Jeannine said calmly, splitting
a lemon neatly, sprinkling each half with salt, and
passing one to Darby.

"What if He comes while we're eating lemons?" Darby asked.

Jeannine shrugged. She was taking the entire thing much more casually than Darby. Darby wasn't sure whether it was because Jeannine had more faith or less. "The important thing is that we're waiting," Jeannine said. "I don't think it matters what else we're doing. Besides, I don't think He'd want us to get bored while we wait."

Darby sank her teeth into the bitter lemon and puckered her face. Even though she liked sour things—lemons, grapefruit, pickles—she could never eat one without feeling like her whole head was shriveling. Looking around again, she searched north, east, south, west, and up. Besides Jesus, she was sure that God would also send a rainbow, as a sign that He had come not to destroy but to save.

"What if He comes from below?" Jeannine said. Jeannine had exasperated Darby during these weeks of discussion by not coming up with any real ideas about how it would happen.

"Below?" The idea had been Darby's own once, but she rejected it now.

"Maybe He's down there talking to the dead in hell," Jeannine suggested. "Giving them one more chance to repent."

Darby scrunched her face as though she'd taken another bite of lemon. It had always been impossible for her to connect a God of love with hell. "I don't believe in hell," she said.

Jeannine shrugged. "You'll see."

The time began to drag. Duchess became impatient and began running up and down the tree, which was her invitation for them to play.

"You stay and watch while I play with Duchess," Jeannine suggested. "Then I'll watch while you play with Duchess."

It sounded like a fine idea to Darby. She wanted to be found faithful, but it would be good to run around a little, too.

For a while, Jeannine played with Duchess under the tree. Then Jeannine took off running around the house, with Duchess in pursuit.

When they disappeared around the corner, Darby suddenly felt abandoned and frightened. She didn't want to face the end of the world alone! Without a glance at the sky or the horizon, she scampered down from the tree and split off after Jeannine and Duchess. Around the house she went, not seeing them until she rounded the last corner and was back in the backyard.

"Where did you go?" Jeannine demanded from up in the tree. "You abandoned the watch!"

"Well, I—"

"What if it had happened while we weren't watching?"

Darby scrambled back into the tree, heart

pounding from the fright and the run, and from being found not watching. What if Jesus had come and she'd been running around the house like a frightened puppy?

"He forgives you," Jeannine said.

"He forgives you, too," Darby said.

"Me? What does He need to forgive me for?" Jeannine sputtered.

"For running off and leaving me," Darby said. "He wouldn't want me to face the end of the world alone."

"You were scared!"

"No, I wasn't."

"You were scared! And all the times we've talked about it, you said you weren't scared."

"Well, I wasn't. And I'm not. But for a minute . . ." Her eyes took another quick inventory of the territory, including down this time. Could He just ease up from the earth like vapors, and could the ground split and crack so they could see the flames of hell? Could the devil follow Him out, and could the tree fall into the pit? She shivered.

"Me, too," Jeannine said. "That's why I ran around the house. I wanted to keep on running and find someplace safe. But I knew that if the world was ending, it would happen wherever I was, so I came on back."

They sat looking at each other. Warmth spread

throughout Darby's body, such a heavenly happiness that she knew it had begun. The end of the world was happening now, and they were alive to see it, and they were faithful and waiting. Once more she looked around—north, east, south, west, up, and down—knowing that when it came it would truly come from all over, all around at once. It would come for her here, for her relatives in Washington and for Yoko, wherever she was. She hoped they were ready, and not afraid.

For a moment it seemed that a cloudy darkness was surrounding them, but the sun was shining still and the sky was blue everywhere. There wasn't a single cloud, and there was no rainbow. There was just herself and Jeannine and Duchess, sitting in the sycamore tree.

They ate lemons until their mouths puckered and searched the sky until their eyes were strained. Then the sun began to set behind Perkerson Park.

"Well, it could end tonight," Jeannine said, a little defensively.

"Sure," Darby said, shrugging her shoulders and trying to squelch her disappointment. "The day isn't really over until midnight."

"No man knoweth," Jeannine said.

Yes, Darby thought, but you acted like you kneweth. But hadn't they had fun, anyway?

Hadn't it been exciting just to think the world was going to end and that they had been faithful?

"You look out your back window, and I'll look out my front window, and it'll be like we're still watching together," Jeannine suggested.

Slowly they climbed down from the sycamore tree, shooing Duchess ahead of them. Any minute their mothers would be calling them. Darby wondered if Jeannine's mother was disappointed.

From the base of the tree, they gathered the lemon rinds they had let fall, and they put them in the garbage can. The world would not end, either before or after midnight, Darby now knew with certainty. If it were going to end at all, it would have ended while they were being faithful and watching. The garbage would still be collected from the cans, and she would go to school on Monday and try once more to say *ma'am* to Miss Hardy. There was still a war. There was still Yoko and Mr. Kaigler, wherever they were. At least LeRoy had his treasured shoes, and she could read the Bible over again, just because she wanted to. There were bad things as well as good, but she was glad to be here.

As she crossed Stewart in the dusk, Darby saw someone in front of Kaigler's, sweeping the sidewalk.

So, they had already sold the store. Yoko and Mr. Kaigler were being made invisible so quickly.

Had she become invisible to all her old friends in Washington? She had written them once, and they had not written back. But she remembered them, the way they looked, the things they'd done together. And how well she remembered Yoko and Mr. Kaigler. She could clearly see Yoko's smooth face and Mr. Kaigler's rough one.

Who was sweeping, she wondered? Who was Mr. Kaigler's replacement? She must not be hateful to the new store owner, any more than she had been to Jeannine. Perhaps he would hire her to sweep. Perhaps, she thought, she would have a panda yet. As curiosity drew her closer to the store, she saw that the man even had on the same kind of white apron that Mr. Kaigler wore, and it encircled a similarly round belly. Whoever he was, she must remember that what had happened was not his fault.

"Eh, *Blümchen,* what you been up to?" the man said, as Darby edged toward Deckner. Startled, she looked up.

"Mr. Kaigler? Mr. Kaigler?" She began running toward him. "Mr. Kaigler! Where have you been?"

"Oh, where I been, eh?" He patted himself on the chest. "Where I been? To see my grandchild into the world, that's where."

"But where have you been?" she demanded.

"Here." He pushed the broom into her hands.

"You're the sweeper. You take the broom, and I'll tell you about my new grandbaby."

Relief weakened the muscles behind Darby's knees. She leaned on the broom for support.

"A little early, she was. In a rush to get here, who knows why. So we had to go quickly. But she's fine and healthy.

"You look pale, *Blümchen*. What you think? You think I'm dead? Is that what you think? Or that they carried me off for a spy, is that what you think?"

Each of his words made her head spin faster. Spies? Did he know what everyone was saying about him, then? She heard her mother calling and she hollered, "Coming."

"Eh, come see, first, before you go. Your mother don't mind for just a minute. I have more new things than grandbaby." He held the door and, when she hesitated, said, "Come, come. I don't eat you! What's this say?" he asked, touching the Colonial Bread sign on the door bar.

"Colonial is good bread," she said, and he closed the door behind them.

"Not Colonel, eh, *Blümchen?*" he said, and she blushed. "Yah. I hear them laugh. But what it matter? People got to have a little fun, eh? Call you Yankee. Soap my windows. So, let them laugh.

They laugh at me plenty and I just say, have a good time."

Everything he said sounded gruff, but the words weren't gruff, and he wasn't gruff. It was just his voice, just the way he was. Darby was so happy, knowing he was safe.

"Hey, Ethel, bring the little Moonbeam," Mr. Kaigler called out, as he led her into the space behind the store. There was a living room, just like a regular house, and no wireless to be seen. "We have his bed in the bathroom," he said to Darby, chuckling.

"Did you know that some people said the world was going to end today?" she asked, suddenly feeling that he, too, was her good friend.

"Ahhch, the world. It ends when it ends," he said. "And what does it matter in the meantime?" A ball of white fluff bounded through the doorway, all tongue and tail. "That's our little Moonbeam," Mr. Kaigler said. "Nice name, eh, *Blümchen?*"

"Oh, she's wonderful!" Darby said. Kneeling, she scooped Greta's puppy into her lap and buried her face in the woolly fur.